Giuseppe Garibaldi

The Rule of the Monk

Rome in the nineteenth century - Vol. 2

Giuseppe Garibaldi

The Rule of the Monk
Rome in the nineteenth century - Vol. 2

ISBN/EAN: 9783337381523

Printed in Europe, USA, Canada, Australia, Japan

Cover: Foto ©Andreas Hilbeck / pixelio.de

More available books at **www.hansebooks.com**

THE

RULE OF THE MONK;

OR,

Rome in the Nineteenth Century.

BY

GENERAL GARIBALDI.

IN TWO VOLUMES.

VOL. II.

CASSELL, PETTER, AND GALPIN,

LONDON AND NEW YORK.

CONTENTS OF THE SECOND VOLUME.

THE RULE OF THE MONK.

CHAPTER XLI.

THE RECLUSE.

In the Italian Archipelago, which may be said to begin in the south at Sicily, and to extend northwards to Corsica, there may be found a nearly deserted island, composed of huge granite crags, down which delicious streams of pure water flow, that never quite fail even in summer. It is rich in vegetation of low but pretty growth, for the tempestuous winds which rush over it prevent the trees from attaining any great height. This, however, is compensated by the healthiness of this little island, in which one may always enjoy fresh and sweet air. The plants that grow out of the crevices in the rocks are chiefly aromatic, and when a fire is made of the leaves and twigs, they send forth a fragrance which perfumes the whole vicinity.

The wandering cattle that graze over the promontories of the island are small in size but very robust. So are, also, the few inhabitants, who live not, indeed, in affluence but in sufficient comfort upon the produce of their tillage, fishing, and shooting, while, moreover, they are supplied with other necessaries from the continent by the gene- rosity or commerce of their friends.

The inhabitants being scanty, police and government are superfluous, and the absence of priests is one of the especial blessings of this little spot. There God is worshipped, as he should be, in purity of spirit, without formalism, fee, or mockery; under the canopy of the blue heavens, with the planets for lamps, the sea-winds for music, and the green sward of the island for altars.

The head of the principal family on this little island is, like other men, one

who has experienced both prosperity and
misfortune.   Like other men he has his
faults, but he has enjoyed the honour
of serving the cause of the people.   Cos-
mopolitan, he loves all countries more or
less ; but Italy and Rome he loves to
adoration.

He hates the priesthood as a lying and
mischievous institution, but is ready, so
soon as they divest themselves of their
malignity and buffoonery, to welcome them
with open arms to a nobler vocation, a
new but honest profession, and to urge men
to pardon their past offences, conforming
in this, as in other acts, to a spirit of
universal tolerance.   Though not suffering
them as priests, he pities and yearns towards
them as men ; for priests he regards as the
assassins of the soul, and in that light
esteems them more culpable than those
who slay the body.   He has passed his
life in the hope of seeing the populations
ennobled and, to the extent of his power,
has championed always and everywhere
their rights, but sadly confesses that he has

lived partly in a false hope; for more than
one nation, raised to freedom and light by
Providence, has paltered again with despotism, whose representatives become perhaps even more unjust and arbitrary than
the patrician.

Still, this man never despairs of the
ultimate amelioration of mankind, albeit
he is deeply grieved at the slowness of its
coming. He regards as the worst enemies
of the liberty of the people those democratic
doctrinaires who have preached and still
preach revolution, not as a terrible remedy,
a stern Nemesis, but as a trade carried on
for their own advancement. He believes
that these same mercenaries of liberty
have ruined many republics, and brought
dishonour upon the republican system. Of
this there is a striking example in the
great and glorious French republic of 1789,
which is held up at the present day as a
scarecrow by despots and their crew against
those who maintain the excellence of the
popular system. He defines a perfect
republic to be a government of honest

and virtuous people by honesty and virtue; and illustrates his definition by pointing to the downfall of all republics when people have eschewed virtue and turned away towards vice. But he does not believe in a republican government composed of 500 governors.

He considers that the liberty of a nation consists in the people choosing their own Government, and that this Government should be dictatorial or presidential—that is to say, directed by one man alone. To such an institution the greatest people in the world owed their greatness. But woe be to those who, instead of a Cincinnatus, elect a Cæsar! The Dictatorship should be limited to a fixed period, and prolonged only in extraordinary cases, such as that of the authority of Abraham Lincoln in the late war of the United States. It must be guarded by popular rights and public opinion from becoming either excessive or hereditary.

The islander whom we are describing, however, is not a dogmatist, and holds that form of Government desired or adopted by

the majority of the people most beneficial
to each nation, and he gives, by way of
illustration, the English constitution. He
regards the existing Continental system as
utterly immoral, and the Governments
guilty of the crimes and suffering that
prevail; since, instead of seeking the
welfare and prosperity of their peoples,
they intrigue only to secure their own
despotic positions. Hence that legion of
armies, political functionaries, and hangers-
on, who devour in idleness the productions
of industry—pampering their vicious appe-
tites, and spreading universal corruption.
These drones of the hive, not content with
what suffices for one man, conspire to appro-
priate to each of themselves the portion of
fifty to maintain their pomp, and supply
their luxuries.

This is just why the working portion of
the populace are loaded with taxes, and
deprived of the manliest of their sons, who
are torn from the plough and the workshop
to swell the ranks of the armies, under the
pretext that they are necessary to their

country's safety, but in reality to sustain a monstrous and fatal form of Government. The people are consequently discontented, starving, and wretched.

The continual state of warfare in which Europe is kept, too clearly shows how ill-governed it is. Were each nation naturally and nobly governed, war would cease, and the people would learn to understand and to respect one another's rights without a passionate or suicidal recourse to arms.

A federation of European nations must be cemented by the medium of representatives for each country, whose fundamental proclamation should be—" War is declared impossible ;" and their second basis the law that " all disputes which may arise between nations shall henceforth be settled by the international congress."

Thus war—that scourge and disgrace of humanity—would be exterminated for ever, and with its extermination, the necessity for maintaining a paid army would obviously cease, and the children of the peoples, now led out to slaughter under the fictitious names of patriotism and glory, would be restored to their families, to the field, and to the workshop, once more to contribute to the fruitfulness and general improvement of their native countries. Such, then, are the sentiments upon these topics of the recluse, and we frankly confess them to be also our own.

To this island, the abode of the recluse, Julia had arranged to take her friends ; but when it became impracticable for Silvia and Clelia to join them, on account of the storm, and the consequent injury to the yacht, she changed her plans, feeling that they would have altered their own, and resolved to touch there only for advice, and then to return to the continent to gain, if possible, some news of Manlio's family.

Picture, courteous reader, one of those Mediterranean daybreaks, which, by its glorious beauty of purple and gold, makes the watchers forget the miseries of life, and ponder only those marvellous marks of the Creator's love with which he has embellished the earth.

Dawn is slowly breaking over the horizon, and tinting with all the colours of the rainbow the fleecy clouds. The stars insensibly pale, and disappear before the radiance of the rising sun, and the voyager stands enchanted at the sight as the gentle breath of morning streams from the east, slightly ruffling the blue waters, and fanning his cheek.

The small ash-coloured island appears in the bright light above the waves, as the *Seagull*, wafted slowly by a slight wind from the eastward, nears its coast. The yacht had sailed from Porto Longone the day before, and had experienced a quick and smooth passage. Her Roman passengers were soon hailed by the inhabitants of the island, as she approached the northern point on this delicious April morning.

The sight of the beautiful yacht was always a welcome one to these dwellers in solitude, for she was well known to them, having previously paid them many visits. They hastened to meet their welcome guest, and ran down to the beach, followed slowly by the head of the family, whose step age and other troubles had slackened, making him no longer able to keep pace with his nimble household.

Julia, upon landing, was welcomed affectionately by all. She introduced her Roman friends, who met a warm reception, and were conducted by their host to his dwelling.

After they had rested some little time, the recluse asked anxiously of Julia, "Well, what news from Rome? Is the foreigner gone yet? Do the priests let the unhappy populace, whom they have tormented so many centuries, breathe free at last?"

"Their miseries are not yet ended," answered the lovely Englishwoman; "and who can tell when they will cease? The foreigner is withdrawn, it is true, but others worse than the first are enlisting, and your Government is shamefully preparing to bribe Italian substitutes to enable it to retain the unhappy city in the power of the priests. Moreover, I, English by birth, but

Italian in heart, am ashamed of telling you
Rome is not to be the capital of Italy.
Government renounces it, and Parliament
basely sanctions the heinous act, to satisfy
the exacting and infamous demands of a
Buonaparte. " Oh, the sadnesses of modern
times ! Italy, once the seat of glory, is
to-day the sink of all that is base. Italy,
the garden of the world, has become a
dunghill ! "

" Oh, Julia ! a people dishonoured is a
dead people. I—even I—almost despair
of the future of such a nation." Thus
exclaimed the leader in many patriotic
battles, as a tear rolled down his cheek.

CHAPTER XLII.

On the day prefixed to this chapter, April, 1849, a foreign sergeant was conducted a prisoner into the presence of the commander of the Gianicolo. He had fallen into a Roman ambuscade during the night time, and having been told by the priests that the defenders of Rome were so many assassins, he threw himself upon his knees as soon as he was taken before them, and begged them for the love of God to spare his life.

The commander extended his right hand to the suppliant, and raising him, spoke comfortingly to him. "This is a good omen," said the Italian officer to those of his companions present. "A good omen! Behold foreign pride prostrate before Roman right — that is a sure sign of victory."

And truly, the foreign army which disembarked at Civita Vecchia, and had fraudulently taken possession of the port, under the deceitfully assumed title of friend, advanced on Rome, chuckling at the credulity, as well as at the cowardice of the Roman people. That very army, afterwards defeated by the native soldiers of the metropolis, re-trod with shame the road to the sea.

The 30th of April was a glorious day for Rome, and was not forgotten among the seven hills. But how could it be commemorated amidst such an armed rabble of enemies ? In the small city of Viterbo, where there were no troops, the inhabitants had devised a way of celebrating the anniversary of the expulsion of the foreigner, and were making active preparations. But if there were no troops there were not wanting spies, who informed the Roman Government of all that took place.

The committee had arranged a programme for the feast, which set forth that after mid-day all work should be suspended, and that all the young people in holiday dress, with a tri-coloured ribbon bound round the left arm, should assemble in the cathedral piazza, and walk thence four abreast in procession to the Porta Romana, so as to pay a salutation of good wishes from that point to the ancient mistress of the globe.

Frightened at this intelligence, the Roman Government despatched to Viterbo in hot haste a body of foreign troops which had only served the priesthood a short time, with orders to suppress the demonstration at any cost. Not heeding this measure the little town held its *festa*, almost forgetting for awhile, in the enjoyment of the moment, her long period of slavery. The solemn salute at the Porta Romana was delivered in spite of the urban authorities, and the procession was returning in good order, preceded by a band playing the national hymns, while the ladies—always more ardent than men in any generous act—stood in the balconies cheering and waving their tri-coloured handkerchiefs to the passers-by, when a column of foreign soldiers was seen advancing at the *pas de charge*, with bayonets fixed. Until now the city, albeit under the rule of the priests, had given herself up with peaceful mirth to the remembrance of that joyful day. But joy fled when the soldiers invaded the streets yet filled with the youthful Viterbians, and anger and trouble succeeded. A delegate of police, who, with a few assistants, preceded the mercenaries, commanded the people to retire. This intimation was received with hisses of defiance; and a few well-aimed stones put them to flight. Taking refuge among the soldiers, they cried out to the troops to fire upon the populace. This command of the cowardly delegate was given because he wished to glut his vengeance, and also to secure a decoration, which he could do by nothing so surely as killing the people. When this inhuman order was not heeded, he feared the hatred between the two opposing parties might cool, and desired the soldiers to charge the populace with fixed bayonets.

The Viterbians, like all Roman citizens, had orders from the Revolutionary Committee not to take active measures of hostility, and were therefore not prepared for the struggle. They dispersed rapidly, and escaped by by-ways to their homes, favoured by the increasing darkness of the evening, as well as by the sudden extinction of all lights, which the women, as if by an universal signal, caused everywhere. Thus the charge of the mercenaries took effect only upon a few stray dogs and dumfounded donkeys on their way home, nor was anything more tragic heard than the barking of the former and the braying of the latter as they were pursued by the valiant champions of the priesthood.

By ten o'clock all was quiet in Viterbo. The troops lay down in the market-place, resting their heads upon their folded arms, preparing to repose upon the laurels won by the fatigues and victory of the day. Not a citizen was to be seen in the streets, all having retired to their houses. At the hotel of the "Full Moon," the bell rang to assemble the guests at a large round table spread with a dinner of about fifty covers. As the bell sounded, a carriage and four drew up to the inn door, and stopping at its gateway, a female clad in travelling costume alighted. From the elasticity of her step and movements it was easy to see she was young. The landlord hastened to receive her, and respectfully enquired whether she would like to be served with supper in her own apartment, to which she replied that she would sup in the public room, and in the meantime her sleeping-room was to be prepared.

The dining-room was already filled with visitors, the greater number of whom were officers belonging to the recently arrived detachment. There were also several strangers, both Italian and foreign, but very few Viterbians present. When the traveller entered the room all eyes were turned towards her with looks of admiration; and truly our Julia, for it was she, appeared very lovely that eventful evening. She possessed to perfection that intelligent

and high-bred expression which distinguishes
her restless race. All made room for her.
The Italians assumed an air of polite admiration, and the officers, twirling the ends
of their pointed moustaches, straightened
their shoulders and adjusted their facial
expression with the look of so many con-
querors of female admiration.

At the head of the table sat the master
of the house, elegantly dressed, who prayed
the beautiful Englishwoman to place herself
by his side. She accepted the seat, and the
officers pressing forward to be near the
young lady, took possession of all the best
places. Observing a Pope's hireling on her
right, Julia began to regret having accepted
the landlord's invitation; and while glancing
round the table with a chagrined air, was
electrified by encountering Muzio's eyes
fixed upon her. He was seated between
Attilio and Orazio at the end of the table.
They all three wore silk hats, cravats, and
overcoats, like foreign travellers, and Julia
had failed to recognise them at first, having
never seen Muzio but when wrapped in his

cloak, or Attilio except in the simple garb
of an artist, and Orazio once only for a
short time in the forest, when armed from
head to foot. What should she do? Rise
and go to them, impulse suggested, and ask
a thousand things which she wished to
know. But how could she venture to do
this, when fifty pairs of eyes were gazing
at her, fascinated by her charming face.

And Muzio, the outcast, the gentleman,
the chief of the counter-police; the man
who, like his namesake (Scavola) would have
placed at his Julia's sweet bidding not his
hand only, but his head also upon burning
coals—what joy the meeting brought, and
yet what agony to see the star of his life,
his goddess, his hope, seated at the side
of a foreign soldier, the instrument of a
vile tyranny, and compelled to accept civili-
ties from his contaminated hand, perhaps
freshly soiled by the blood of Romans.
Oh, you young men, who are in love
with a noble maiden, have you not felt
what splendid new strength her presence
gives to you! When unworthy men pre-

sume to affront her with attentions, at such a
moment do you not feel you have ten hearts
to devote to her, ten men's lives to sacrifice
for her? If not, you are a coward; and
a coward, let us tell you, is despised by
women.

You may sin, and she will pardon you;
but cowardice a noble woman will never
forgive. Muzio, however, was only too
loving and rash; and woe to that fine lady-
killer by the British maiden's side! Had
the Roman youth yielded to the dictates
of his angry breast, it wanted little to have
seen a flash of fire in the air, or to have
let him feel the cold blade of a dagger in
his vitals.

But Julia read in her lover's eye the
storm that was raging, and her look, perceived by him alone, calmed down the
Roman's passionate soul.

Between the courses, the foreign officers
conversed on the affairs of Rome, or the
topics of the day, and, as usual, with but
little respect for the Roman people, whom
they commonly despised. Julia, disgusted

by their indecorous conversation, rose very
soon, with a majestic mien, and desired to
be conducted to her apartment. Our three
friends were burning to kiss her hand, and
had even made a move to quit their places,
when a sudden burst of laughter from the
foreign officers made them resume their
seats. The laughter was caused by a
coarse jest, uttered by one of the number,
of which the following words came to the
ears of our indignant trio:—"I thought I
was coming to Viterbo to use my arms
against men, but find there are only
rabbits here, who bolted into their burrows
at our very appearance. Diavolo! where
are all these Liberals who make such a
noise?"

Attilio, who had not reseated himself,
hastily gathered his own and his friends'
gloves, and, making them into a handful,
threw them, without a word, full and hard
in the face of the slanderer.

"Oh!" exclaimed the Papalino; "what
bundle is here?" and picking up the
missile, he unrolled the gloves, saying,

" So, then, I am challenged by three! Here is another sample of Italian valour! Three against one! three against one!" And again the fellow laughed immoderately.

The three allowed this fresh burst of merriment to pass, but the hilarity of all the strangers present being aroused by it, Muzio, as soon as the laughter ceased, cried in a loud voice, "Three against as many as dare to insult Italians, gentlemen!"

The effect of these few words was very startling, for, as he uttered them, the three friends arose and darted angry glances first at one and then at another of the officers, presenting, with their uncovered and bold young heads to the assembly, three models à la Michael Angelo. They were three variations of that manly and martial beauty which nature's heroes have; three types of noble anger in the glowing veins of generous courage.

Different effects were produced on the two parties present. The Italians at the table were delighted, and regarded the champions of Italian honour with smiling approbation and gratitude.

The foreigners remained for a time stupefied, wondering at the personal grace and manly beauty of the trio, and at their nervous and proud bearing. This amazement ended, sarcasm came to the rescue, and one of the youngest exclaimed, " Friends, a toast!" All rose, glass in hand, and he continued: "I drink to the fortune of having at last found enemies worthy of us in this country!"

Orazio responded, "I drink to the liberation of Rome from foreign filth."

These words seemed to the officers to be too insulting to be overlooked, and they placed their hands menacingly upon their swords; but one of the number, of a maturer age, said gravely, " My friends, it will not answer to make a disturbance here. The peace of the city must not be disturbed, for we came here to restore order. At daybreak we will meet in even numbers these quarrelsome signors. What we have to do is to see that they do not then deprive us of the honour of meeting them.

"The opportunity of fighting the enemies of Italy is much too happy a circumstance to let it escape," answered Attilio. "If it please you we will remain together until morning, when we can walk in company to the place of meeting."

To this proposition all consented. The foreigners called for writing materials, to inscribe their names, in order to draw lots to decide who should fight. Amongst the Italians three gentlemen offered to be seconds to their countrymen. Then there were the arms to be considered. As there had been such open defiance on both sides, it was decided that they should fight to the death, that the opponents should be placed at a distance of fifteen paces apart, and that at a signal from their seconds they should attack one another with sabre, revolver, and poniard.

The three champions of the priests whose names, written upon slips of paper, were drawn out of the hat which served the purpose of an urn, were Foulard, a French Legitimist; Sanchez, a Spanish Carlist; and Haynau, an Austrian. The seconds busied themselves during the remainder of the night in examining the arms, and in endeavouring to match them with absolute equality.

CHAPTER XLIII.

THE COMBAT.

THE morning of the 1st of May was dawning over the top of the Ciminian wood—now called Monte di Viterbo—when twelve persons, wrapped in their cloaks, traversed the steep road which crosses it, and disappeared among the trees. They proceeded in silence till they reached an eminence, which overlooked a part of the wood, when Attilio, addressing the Italians, said, "Here, in this forest, the last advocates of Etruscan independence sought refuge, beaten and pursued by our fathers, the Romans; and here, in one of the last battles, they disappeared from among the Italian tribes—the most ancient, the most famous, and the most gifted people of the peninsula."

Captain Foulard, who understood Italian sufficiently to comprehend Attilio's speech, and to whom it was indirectly addressed, replied, " I fancy it was here, or hereabouts, too, that my ancestors, the Gauls, fought those famous battles with your Roman forefathers, who would have disappeared from the face of the earth had it not been for the hissing of their geese."

Attilio, though incensed, answered calmly, " When your forefathers crept on all fours in the forests of Gaul, `our ancestors dragged them out, and made them stand upon their legs, saying, 'Be human creatures.' Your modern politeness shows but little gratitude to your former civilisers. But we came here not to dispute, but to fight."

The place at which they had just arrived was one of those pleasant glades, devoid of trees, which Nature often hides in the heart of an Italian forest, and which she adorns prodigally with lavish though concealed beauties. That tranquil and enchanting spot was, however, now to become the scene of fury and of bloodshed, for, the position being chosen, and the fifteen paces measured, the six seconds retired, after exchanging a few words with their respective companions.

The adversaries were standing ready to rush upon each other. The first and second signals had been given, and six angry hearts were impatiently awaiting the third, when a trumpet was heard sounding the advance, and immediately there appeared in sight, marching along the road by which the opponents had come, a company of the Pope's foreign soldiers, followed by the delegate Sempronio, and a few of his subordinates.

And here we must in justice confess that the officers, though mercenaries, were much mortified by this occurrence, and almost on the point of defending their adversaries, and of helping them to escape, when the command was given by the delegate to the troops to surround the Italians with fixed bayonets.

To ordinary persons such an order would have sounded like the knell of all hope, and a hasty flight, if flight had yet seemed possible, would have been the one remaining idea; but our Romans were men to sustain any shock or peril, however abrupt, without losing in the least their presence of mind. At the first sound of the trumpet they cast their eyes on their antagonists, and saw with satisfaction, by their unfeigned surprise, that those gentlemen had no previous knowledge of the approaching cowardly attack, and then, facing their assailants, they retired without haste, revolver in hand, towards the forest.

The troops, perceiving with wonder, upon their arrival, that some of their own officers were among the persons they had been directed to arrest, paused for a moment, uncertain how to act. Sempronio, who had cautiously placed himself behind them, seeing the untoward result of what he had been pleased to term his plan of battle, became furious, and shouted loudly, " Fire — fire on that side ! on that side !" pointing to his own countrymen, for whose blood he thirsted, as they slowly retired towards the cover, which having gained, they turned and faced the troops.

The soldiers still paused, but the delegate's nearest associates fired then and there upon the six Italians, and, although screened by the wood, two of the seconds were slightly hit. Attilio's revolver speedily avenged his wounded companions. His shot had the fortune to pass directly through the nose of Father Sempronio (for he was a priest disguised as an agent), carrying away the bridge of it.

It was a stroke of luck indeed. Sempronio's cries and terrible lamentations aroused more contempt than pity, for the latter is rarely expended upon creatures of his despicable character. Roaring and bleeding, the priest-delegate took to his heels, and ran back to Viterbo, leaving to the others the execution of his "plan of battle."

The foreign officers were nearly all ashamed of the ugly position in which they were placed, though the delegate, and not they, had planned the surprise. The

discovery of their names had been made
by a spy, and the excited Sempronio had
trusted in this easy manner to secure a
batch of proscribed Italians, and carry them
prisoners to Rome, in hopes of helping
himself towards a cardinal's hat.

Sempronio had men like himself among
his force less scrupulous than the six
duellists, especially a certain Captain Tortiglio, the commander of the company,
another cold-blooded Carlist, who thought
it would be an easy matter to get to the
end of it by capturing the proscribed, as
they were so few in number. He* accordingly resolved to follow them into the
forest.

Our friends, having prayed the wounded
to escape deeper into the thicket, still
fronted their enemies as long as they had
any shots left, and for a time, being protected by the trees, they managed to hold
their assailants at bay. But when their
ammunition was nearly gone they were
obliged to retire before the soldiers, who
were urged on by the Captain's "Voto a

Dios," and "Carambas," as he followed, swearing he would capture "these scoundrels," whose arrest, doubtless, would bring him no small reward from the Papal Government.

Fortunately, Orazio had with him his inseparable horn, and drawing it forth, he blew the same blast which was heard on his arrival at the Castle of Lucullus. No sooner had the echo died away, than a sound as of many steps was heard.

The footsteps were those of the companions of Orazio—a portion of the Three Hundred who had re-united in the Ciminian forest, after the occurrences at Rome already described. They had been awaiting the return to the rendezvous of their leaders, who had been absent a few days in Viterbo, upon important business.

But who are they who precede the band appearing so opportunely on the scene of action? Who are those graceful commanders? None other than Clelia and Irene, like the Amazons of old, and at their side is the intrepid Jack, burning to "do his duty" and be of use in such beautiful company.

The proscribed, at this welcome accession of strength, did not discharge a single shot, but, fixing their bayonets, charged the foreign mercenaries, with the cry of "Viva l'Italia!" and dispersed them as the torrent disperses twigs and leaves in its headlong course. The soldiers, terrified at the sudden increase of numbers on the side of the enemy, and by the furious onset, turned and fled at full speed, regardless of the threats of their officers, and even the slashes made at them with sabres.

Captain Tortiglio, who was not wanting in courage, had rushed in advance of his men, and now stood all alone. He was very much mortified, but disdained to run away. Attilio was the first to come up to him, and summoned him to surrender.

"No," cried Tortiglio, " I will not surrender."

Attilio, wrapping his cloak around his left arm, put aside the captain's sword, as he dealt a savage blow at him, and sprang

upon him, holding his poniard in his right
hand. The Spaniard was small of stature,
yet very agile in his movements. He struggled for some time, but the young sculptor
finally lifted him by main force from the
ground, and, provoked by the resistance of
the manikin, yet not wishing to kill him,
gave him an overturn upon the ground, as
a cook serves a pan-cake. Happily for Tortiglio the soil was covered with turf, or not
all the science of Æsculapius would have
sufficed to re-set his broken bones.

The proscribed pursued the soldiers only
to the further edge of the meadow, where
they contented themselves with a few part-
ing shots, and then turned their attention
to the wounded of both sides. Those of the
enemy they sent to Viterbo, under the escort
of the prisoners, and despatched their own
to the interior of the wood, but retained
Captain Tortiglio a little while, more as a
hostage than a prisoner. Clelia and Irene
were praised and complimented by all
for their promptitude and courage. Muzio,
after kissing their hands, made them a little

speech of victory: "It becomes you well,
brave and worthy daughters of Rome," he
said, "to set such an example to our companions, but more especially to the slothful
among Italy's sons, who appear to expect
the manna of freedom to fall from heaven,
and basely await their country's liberation
at the hand of the foreigner. They are not
ashamed to kiss the rod of a foreign tyrant,
patron, and master; to renounce their own
Rome—the natural and legitimate metropolis of Italy—voted the capital by parliament, and desired by the whole nation.
They are not ashamed to let her remain a
den of priests, of creatures who are the
scourge and the shame of humanity. To
women! yes, to women, is descended the
task of extirpating this infamy, since men
are afraid or incapable of doing it."

Muzio, at this point in his vehement
oration in honour of the fair sex, was suddenly struck dumb by the apparition of
another representative of it in the form of
a lovely woman, with the face and carriage,
as he afterwards said, of an angel of heaven,

who appeared to him to have fallen from
the clouds, and was standing before him on
the road leading to Viterbo. His eloquence
vanished, and he remained motionless as a
statue, although the very silence of the
youth showed that he recognised her to be
the adored queen of his heart, English
Julia.

Muzio's embarrassment was the less no-
ticed because of Jack's headlong demonstration, for the sailor, with a hitch at his
waist-band, sprang forward towards his beautiful mistress, throwing at the same time
even his precious carbine on the ground,
which he never would have abandoned under
any other circumstances for all the surprises
in the universe. When he at last reached
Julia, he nearly plucked his forelock out by
the root, so perpetually and persistently did
he twitch at it, saluting the English lady.
Poor fellow! a thousand affections and re-
membrances of family, friends, and country
were centred for him in the person of that
beloved mistress. Julia took the English
boy's hand gracefully and kindly, and Clelia

and Silvia embraced her with transports of
friendship, and then presented her to Irene,
whose romantic history had been repeated
to her, and whom she had much desired to
know personally.

Even the followers of Orazio forgot for a
moment their discipline, and crowded around
this charming daughter of Albion, gazing
at her with looks of undisguised admiration. Woman as she was, Julia could
not but feel a thrill of pride and pleasure
at the homage of these bold and honest
children of Italy.

CHAPTER XLIV.

THE OLD OAK.

AFTER receiving the more formal salutations of Attilio and Orazio, Julia did not forget to turn for a little towards her lover, who had remained during all these demonstrations somewhat eclipsed and confused.

Muzio, even when a child of the streets, had always maintained that decorum of person and propriety of manner which the remembrance of his noble birth imposed upon him; and now Julia had reason indeed to admire the change wrought in him by his life in the forest.

The position of the last scion of the house of Pompeo had truly improved of late. Scipio, the faithful and devoted servant who had voluntarily taken charge of him when a baby, and tended him with such devoted affection, was dead; but before dying, he imparted, by writing, to Cardinal S——, Muzio's maternal uncle, the history of his young master's life, and a statement of his family property. The prelate gave his solicitor orders to put himself in communication with Muzio, to supply him with all he needed, and to endeavour to bring him back into the sheep-fold of respectability.

The prelate, moreover, had kindly intentions towards his nephew on his own part, and meditated adding something from his own possessions to the paternal estates which had passed so fraudulently into the hands of Paolotti's vultures, and which he saw the way to recover.

This sudden change of fortune happened to Muzio about the end of the year 1866, in which the Italians, in spite of the undesirable means used, gained re-possession of their own soil, and got rid of the foreign friends of the priesthood.

It was, therefore, not an untimely thing for Cardinal S—— to be able to say, " I

have a nephew who is a Liberal, and one
of the first temper, too;" for it became
of consequence, even to a prelate, to be on
friendly terms with such a nephew.

Julia contemplated the transformation
of Muzio's appearance and apparel with
natural pleasure, yet she had loved him
so much as a wanderer of the city, that
she almost wished him back again in the
poor but graceful cloak of a Trastevere
model.

Muzio made no audible reply to his lady's
gentle words of recognition, but kissed her
hand with a devotion that needed no speeches
to mark its intensity, and which could not
be better translated than by his enamoured
mistress's heart.

And Clelia and Irene were, of course,
happy at being once more safe in the society
of their chosen. Happiness was depicted
upon all these youthful faces; and, in truth,
it is necessary to confess that, opposed as all
good hearts are to bloodshed, the hour of
victory is a glorious one, and we, like many
others, have enjoyed that wild and stern

delight. At such a moment the mind,
perhaps, is not so prone to reflect on the
sad fact that the field is covered with the
wounded and the dying. Their cries and
our own exhaustion are alike unheeded. We
are victorious; our cause has conquered.
We have routed the enemy. All meetings on
the field take a joyous tone from that proud
thought; and every fresh friend, as he comes
up, receives a hearty squeeze of the hand,
and is a centre of fresh congratulations.

Brothers have killed brothers. Yes,
alas! Manzoni is right! but the heart of
man forgets that sad verity so long as the
flush of victory is cast upon it. Ah! when
will the people become brethren indeed,
and exchange the savage bliss of triumph
for the noble and placid joys of peace?
Ere long, let us hope! So, be sure, hoped
and prayed that band, under an ancient oak,
upon the emerald sod of the forest, where
the chiefs of the proscribed sat with those
noble and tender women whose strange fate
had brought them together on the field
of battle. They were so beautiful, so

attractive, to be in such a place! With
faces kindled by pride and love, they spread
around them a light of joy and a sense
of praise and admiration; an atmosphere
of grace mingled with gallant spirit, which
almost rendered their companions eager to
fight again and again under such glorious
eyes.

Silvia was the first to break the thread of
felicitations, as she enquiringly said to Julia,
"But Manlio, where did you leave him?"

"Manlio," replied the Englishwoman, "is
with the Recluse on the island; I left him
in excellent health, and promised to take
him news of you."

"And what is the General's opinion con-
cerning affairs in Rome?" asked Attilio.

"He," replied Julia, "approves of the
noble conduct of the few Romans' who
harass the Papal Government, and who protest to the world by their rebellion, that that
abomination is no longer compatible with
the age; yet he applauds also the endurance with which you have waited for a general movement until now, so as not to trouble

the advancement of national unity, thus depriving the foreigner of a pretext to create
further obstacles. But at the same time he
is of opinion that as long as the Italian
Government continues to remain kneeling
at the feet of the Master of France, and, to
please him, renounces Rome as the capital
of our fatherland—while it supports the
wicked priesthood—you must be ready to
decide these questions by arms, and that
every man in Italy who possesses an Italian
heart ought to be prepared to support
you."

"Yes," said Muzio, who had been mut-
tering the word "endurance" ever since
it was spoken by Julia—"yes, but patience
is the virtue of the ass. We Romans
have had too much of it; we have been,
and still are superabundantly asinine. It
is a disgrace to us that we still tolerate the
most iniquitous and degrading of human
tyrannies, and suffer the priests to be our
gaolers."

"And is this island from which you
come far off?" enquired the gentle Silvia,

who was thinking most about the dear companion of her life. " Could we not go and pass a few days there?"

" Nothing is easier," answered Julia, to whom the question was put. " We are close to the frontier, we have only to cross it, and make our way to Leghorn, where the *Seagull* is lying, and sail from thence to the island, which is not far distant. But you must also know of the marriage of Captain Thompson and your friend Aurelia, which took place lately in that solitary retreat in the simple patriarchal manner, for there are no priests there."

" *Per la grazia di Dio !* " here exclaimed Orazio to himself, rising and stretching his athletic figure to its full height, as he cast a look to the western extremity of the wood. " What are these fresh arrivals? " whereupon they all saw advancing towards them a robust youth, accompanied by a beautiful girl, not much his junior, but upon whose melancholy face the traces of suffering and misfortune were too plainly visible.

The new-comers were quickly perceived

to be Silvio and Camilla; and here it should
be known that our hunter, after the de-
cision of the Liberals to abandon the Roman suburbs, went to bid farewell to his
unhappy mistress, whom he could not cease
to love, before setting out for the north.

Arriving at Marcello's house, he was welcomed as usual by Fido and Marcellino, and
found Camilla kneeling, as was her daily
habit, beside her father's grave.

"Just God! can another's crime plunge a
simple and innocent soul into misery and
madness for life?" thought Silvio, as he
regarded the prostrate girl, and almost un-
consciously he prayed aloud, "Oh, heaven!
restore her reason, and to me the star of
my life!"

Camilla turned at these words with a look
first of fright, then of a new and wonderful
tenderness. It was plain that that compas-
sionate and forgiving prayer had caused the
inmost fibres of her heart to vibrate, and,
obeying a mighty and impulsive instinct,
she sank into the old sweet sanctuary of her
lover's arms. With their heads hidden on

each other's breasts, they dispensed with explanations—they made no new vows—mighty love was healer and interpreter. Tears fell fast from Camilla's eyes, but not sad tears now. A great sorrow and a bitter sin had dethroned her reason—a great pardon and a noble love set it back again in its happy seat.

CHAPTER XLV.

THE new arrivals were received with surprise and pleasure by our forest party. The signoras were all conversant with the history of Camilla's misfortunes, and bestowed upon her gentle and considerate caresses. Something solemn pervaded her whole appearance—a dreamy vestige of the insanity under which she had so long laboured. It was a miraculous change which had come over her when she heard that pathetic prayer, and perceived the sudden presence of her lover, and the unutterable feelings of affection and penitence that stirred her soul when she found herself restored to his embrace had transformed her into a new and happy being, but left upon her this air of mystic pathos.

"I passed through Viterbo," said Silvio

to Orazio, when their salutations were ended,
"and saw a great commotion there for which
I am scarcely able to account. The citizens
were running about the streets, endeavouring
to get out of the way of the soldiers. The
soldiers, reinforced by strong detachments
from Rome, are vowing to spear all Italians
on the face of the earth, and, by way of a
step towards this warlike project, have begun plundering the wine-shops, where many
for the most part lie dead drunk. The
Papal authorities, who wished to keep the
peace, were received by the rascals with the
butt-ends of their muskets, and driven to
flight. They have gone off with their
agents to Rome, and are not likely to return
for some time. The reinforcements were
exclaiming that 'their flag had been dishonoured, and that the stain must be
washed out in blood.' 'Flag dishonoured!'
that phrase calls to our mind the villany
of a certain neighbouring Government,
which, after infamously violating our territory, and taking, by a deceitful act, possession of our principal sea-port, treacherously

attacked our capital, and upon receiving some severe blows, cried out 'Treason! treason! our flag is dishonoured!'"

"But," said Silvio, resuming his narrative, "this confusion gave me a favourable opportunity of making observations, and coming on quietly to you, though I might have been hindered by a curious occurrence which happened. I was passing the 'Full Moon' hotel as a few officers, newly arrived from Rome, alighted from a carriage. Owing to the universal confusion, they could find no attendant to carry in their luggage, and one of them came up to me, crying out, 'Here, you fellow!' and taking me by the breast, attempted to drag me to the carriage. Fortunately I had already signalled to Camilla to go on in advance of me. My first impulse was to use my poniard, but restraining myself, I tore the man's hand from my breast, and aiming a blow with my fist full at his face, sent him flying against the wheels of the carriage without a single word. As you may imagine, I did not remain to gather the laurels of the victory,

but turned on my heel, and walked with a
quick step in the direction of the wood, and
soon overtook my companion."

The merriment of his auditors, and the
shouts of " Bravo, Silvio ! " here interrupted
the narrator for a moment.

" However," he observed, when the laughter ceased, " we cannot remain long here in
security, for I have no doubt that to-morrow,
at latest, you will have the whole pack of
foreigners on your track."

" Here in this forest," said Orazio, " we
could make head against the whole army of
the Pope, were it not that we are so very
few in number, and have these precious
ladies to protect."

" Ehi ! ladies to protect, indeed ! " said
Irene with some irony ; " you have soon
forgotten, Signor Rodomonte, that these
same ' ladies ' protected you to-day."

A burst of laughter broke from all ; and
the courageous chief of the forest stooped
and kissed the hand of his beloved wife with
pretty submission.

Meanwhile, the long dark shadows cast

by the giants of the Ciminian wood spreading out to the west announced the setting of the sun, who, wrapped in a glorious and variegated mantle of clouds, was about to hide himself behind the waves of the Tyrrhenian sea. Clelia, perceiving this, addressed Jack, who, fascinated by her beauty and amiability, was her devoted slave, and to whom she had confided the important care of the viands. "Well, my friend," she said in English, "all these true heroes of romance, it appears, do not trouble themselves about supper; and if you do not see to it, I fear we shall have to go to bed without food to-night."

"Aye, aye, ma'am!" was Jack's reply; and, with the invariable hitch to his waistband, he steered for the spot where the assistants had unloaded two mules, which carried the chief's baggage as well as the provisions. But, after such fighting and talk, they must feast at leisure in a fresh chapter.

CHAPTER XLVI.

THE RURAL SUPPER.

WHO does not prefer civilisation to barbarism and the usages of savage life? Who would not choose the comforts of a refined home, cool in summer, warm in winter, well supplied with food, and replete with every comfort and even luxury, to the open country, with its inclemency, inconveniences, and vicissitudes of weather?

Yet when one remembers that the few monopolise the advantages of civilisation, and that its victims are so many, one cannot help doubting whether the world of humanity does reap much benefit from the present highly-developed state of civilisation, and whether it might not be desirable to go back to the simple condition of the first inhabitants of the world, amongst whom, if there were no palaces, no cooks, no fine manners, no expensive clothes, no elaborate conventions, no luxuries in the way of food, neither were there any priests, police, pre- fects, tax-gatherers, or any other of our galling modern innovations; neither was one called upon to give up one's children to serve the caprices of a despot, under the pretence of serving the country and washing out "stains from flags."

However all this may be, a frugal supper in the forest on the soft green turf, hitherto untrodden by any foot of man; the guests seated on the trunks of old trees that fur- nish also a glowing and dancing fire; by the side, moreover, of such companions as Julia, Clelia, and Irene—a supper in such circumstances must be a more delightful scene of enjoyment than civilisation could afford. *Per Dio!* give us such a forest supper, though it consist only of fruit and the luck of the chase, against any grand in-door entertainment. Many a time have we shared such a repast.

But our forest party had more than meagre fare. Gasparo, who was also in charge of the baggage, was commissioned, in company with Jack, to purchase and look after the provisions. He now spread a cold collation before the chiefs, with the sailor-boy's assistance—garnishing it with some green branches—which would have tempted even the palate of a Lucullus.

A few flasks of Montepulciano and Orvieto embellished the enamelled table, and, the savoury viands, seasoned with the appetite which follows an arduous day's work, disappeared with amazing rapidity.

Julia was in high spirits. It was the first time she had shared in such a *fête-champêtre*, in the society, above all, of those who were her *beau ideal* of all that was romantic, chivalrous, and gallant.

Very near to her was her Muzio, disguised in the garb of a Roman model, and who was now known and proclaimed to be the descendant of an ancient noble family, and one of the richest heirs in Rome it might yet appear.

That resistless principle, which, like the load-stone and the needle, attracts loving souls one to the other, kept him at the side

of the woman of his heart, watching her
slightest wish, providing her with everything with proud servility; and all the
while, humbly glancing at her with that
look which art vainly seeks to represent—
the look which alone can be given and
understood between those who love with
a true and perfect love.

Julia also, with a little graceful dignity,
enjoyed hearing Clelia and Irene converse
with Jack in broken Italo-English. They
drew him out to relate some of the episodes
of his sea-life, the adventures he had met
with, and the tempests he had witnessed in
his long voyages to India and China, for he
had been at sea since he was seven years
old. The description he gave of the Chinese
who stay at home and employ themselves
in different kinds of work performed by
women in other countries, while their wives
row, and till the land, with their babies
slung in a basket on their backs, caused
much laughter among his fair hearers, and,
indeed, to all present, when translated to
them by one of the company.

" The nautical profession," said Julia, " is
the one to which my country is most in-
debted for her greatness. My countrymen
prize and honour their mariners. With us,
not only in the countries bordered by the
sea, but wherever there is a river or a lake,
boys are to be seen continually taking exercise in boating and rowing, in which prac-
tices they run all kinds of danger, and this
is the reason there are so many seafaring
men to make the name of Britain great
upon the ocean."

" I have known youths in France and
Italy, who were destined to become naval
officers, pass the greater part of their boyhood in the technical schools, going on
board for the first time when they had
attained their fifteenth and even their
eighteenth year, when they suffer much,
of course, from sea-sickness, and are exposed to the ridicule and contempt of the
sailors.

" In England it is very different. Youths
destined for the sea are put on board at
eleven years of age, and frequently take

long voyages, during which they are instructed practically in all the routine and details of their profession. This course insures the best naval officers in the world to England.

"The wealthy among my people do not hoard up money to look at it, but employ it frequently in purchasing a yacht; and there are, indeed, very few persons living near sea or river who do not own or hire some sort of craft, large or small, in which they take their pleasure, and exercise themselves in the art which constitutes the glory and prosperity of their land.

"In Italy you have seamen, I grant, who equal the best of any nation, but your officers will not stand the test of comparison. Your Ministers of Marine have ever been incompetent, and therefore incapable of improving and raising a profession which might yet render Italy one of the most important and prosperous nations of the globe."

The subject so treated by Julia was a little foreign to our Romans, who were

naturally ignorant of sea affairs. Their
priests long ago found the oar and the net
of St. Peter far too heavy for their effeminate
hands, and gave themselves up to merry-
making and luxury as the easiest way of
promoting the glory of God.

A pause here ensuing, Julia called for a
song or narrative, and Orazio said, "Gasparo,
the chief of bandits, could tell us, doubtless, some stirring passages in his adventurous life." Whereupon, with a bow
and smile, the old man sate for a moment
recalling some circumstance of his past life,
and then answered—

"Perils on the sea I could not relate,
because I have been very little upon it;
but on land I have passed through my
share of strange adventures; and if it will
not weary you to listen to one, I could,
perhaps, relate events that would make
you shudder."

All expressing a wish to hear some
portion of his history, Gasparo, settling
himself down in an easy attitude, commenced the following story.

CHAPTER XLVII.

"I was born in the small city of S——, in the States of the Church, not far from the Neapolitan frontier. My parents were honest folk, employed as shepherds in the service of the Cardinal B——.

"Being sent early to the field to tend sheep, cows, and buffaloes, and nearly always on horseback, I grew up with a robust hardy constitution, and became a dexterous horseman.

"Up to the age of eighteen, I remained a true son of the Italian desert, knowing no other affection than that which I had for my horse, my lasso, and my weapons. With the latter I had become a formidable enemy to the deer and wild boar of the Roman forests. I was passionately fond of hunting, an exercise suited to my nature;

and I was accustomed to pass whole nights
lying in ambush, watching for the deer,
or the great grey tuskers in the marshes,
where they delight to lie rolling in
the mud.

"I knew the places frequented by the
harts and hinds, and very often returned
home with one of those graceful animals
slung over my saddle.

"One day, after having secured my horse
at a little distance, I placed myself in
hiding, on the watch for a stag. I had
been there but a short time, when I heard
footsteps on the path behind me—a narrow
forest road that led to the village.

"At first I thought it might be a wild
beast of some description, and kept my
carbine in readiness to fire as soon as
I perceived it. After listening a few
moments, I thought I heard voices, and
presently there appeared in sight a young
priest whom I had occasionally seen
walking in the village, while by his side
was a young girl who appeared to accompany him rather unwillingly.

"I had time to observe them both; the priest was about twenty years of age, very tall and finely proportioned; in fact, only a carbine and pointed hat were wanting to make a fine hunter or soldier of him."

"The young girl! Ah! pardon my memory, still agitated by that sweet face!" and the old man's eyes here dimmed with tears. "The young girl was an angel! I do not know how it was they did not discover me, for her beauty caused me to utter an involuntary exclamation, and my heart was stirred by a new and astonishing emotion.

"He had offended her by some proposal, for she was turning to go; but as I regarded them, the priest threw his arm with almost violent force around his companion, and pressing his lips to her cheek, uttered some words that did not reach me, but caused a terrified and indignant look to pass over the girl's face, and she shrank back as if stung by a viper. Again the priest spoke and approached, when, with a cry, the peasant-girl broke from him and fled.

" He pursued her, and caught the shriek-
ing damsel, whose hands he bound with her
neck-ribbon, and then forced her upon the
ground. I cannot tell why I was self-con-
tained enough not to shoot him dead, but I
had never drawn trigger against a human
life, and I hesitated until he gave these last
proofs of his abominable villainy. At this
point, however, I sprang from my covert,
and with one blow from the butt-end of my
gun, felled him to the ground, and then
went to the assistance of the young woman,
who had fallen fainting at some little distance upon the sod. I raised her gently in
my arms, and carried her to the side of a
brook, where I bathed her face with the
cool, running water, until she opened her
lovely eyes and faintly smiled her thanks,
for, as she gazed around, a look of relief
passed over her features, when she perceived
the absence of her persecutor. Then rising,
she expressed, in a few words, her gratitude
for my intervention, saying she was sufficiently recovered to return to the village, and
bade me farewell, but seeing she was still

agitated, I begged her to allow me to conduct her to her home. She gave a modest
assent, and I walked in happy and respectful
silence till we reached the entrance to the
village, where she stopped, and pointing to
a small but pretty dwelling, said, 'That is
my father's house; I have nothing more now
to fear, so I will bid you a grateful adieu.'
Raising her hand to my lips, I kissed it
fervently, saying, I hoped to have the
pleasure of meeting her soon again, under
calmer circumstances, for I was completely
enchanted by her grace and beauty, and felt
I could no longer be happy out of her
presence.

"I remained to watch her enter her
abode before I turned to seek my horse,
which I found neighing impatiently at
my prolonged absence. Through some acquaintances in the village, I ascertained the
name of her whom I had been the means
of saving from violence, and learned to my
disappointment and horror that she was the
priest's niece. Day after day, I found some
pretext for passing through the village, that

I might obtain a glimpse of Alba, for that
was her name; and twice I was fortunate
enough to meet her and exchange a few
words. I did not speak to her of love, but
I felt she knew my passion for her, and
was trying to return it.

"The priest, burning with rage at the
thought of his infamy being not only frustrated by me but made known to the father
of the maiden, resolved to be revenged.
Being reproved by the old man for his
brutal conduct, and threatened with public
exposure, unless he absented himself for a
long time, until he should have thoroughly
repented of his intended crime, the priest
fell upon the old man, and with one blow
from a mallet crushed in his skull. Then,
fearing the consequences, he carried the
dead body into the court-yard, and,
placing it upon its back near a rugged
stone, left it there, and retired to bed,
leaving his neighbours to suppose, when
the corpse was discovered in the morning,
that the old man had fallen down in
a fit, and striking his head against the

stone pavement, had thus met with his death."

What matters a crime to a priest, if he can cover it? He had committed a gross lie by calling himself the minister of God, and now he took advantage of the easy ignorance of his neighbours to conceal a still grosser crime.

Those of his profession use double dealing all their lives. A priest knows himself to be an impostor, unless he be a fool, or have been taught to lie from his boyhood, so that as he advances in years, he becomes not even able any longer to dissociate the false and the true. Whilst he lives in comfort, he makes the credulous multitude believe he suffers hardships and privations. Poor priest! Well do we remember seeing in America a painting representing one of the cloth seated at a dining-table spread with all kinds of viands and a flagon of wine, in the act of caressing his plump and rosy Perpetua, who was seated at his side; and, meanwhile, outside the door stood a poor Irishman with his wife and baby. All

three were wan, emaciated, and miserably
clad, yet the husband was dropping a coin
into the priest's box, on which was written,
" Give of your charity to the poor priest of
God." Infamous mockery! On the one hand
there was plenty, enjoyment, hypocrisy, and
lying; on the other, poverty, ignorance, credulity, and innocent misery.

"One evening," continued Gasparo, "I
was sitting in my hut, feeling rather weary
after a long day's hunt, thinking of Alba,
and dreading, from what she had told me,
that some catastrophe might be impending,
when the door flew open, and the object
of my thoughts rushed in exclaiming,
'Murder! Murder!' and fell insensible
upon the floor.

CHAPTER XLVIII.

"The words of Alba revealed to me the horrible crime that had been perpetrated. I raised her fainting form, and laid her upon my pallet, for my parents were both dead, and I dwelt alone. Now I could, for the first time, realise the full and sweet beauty of my heart's love. The sight of this lovely creature almost lessened my aversion to the vile homicide and his unlawful passion. Alba had never related to me what had passed on that night, and as I did not wish to awaken painful recollections, I had always avoided interrogating her upon the subject, so that I knew nothing of the dispute and murder. But the priest, supposing me aware of his misdeeds, and jealous of my love for Alba, schemed, as only a fiend could, to anni-

F 2

hilate me through his own crime, though
not daring to accuse me openly. He had
hinted to his most intimate friends that
I was the murderer, and offered all he
possessed to certain bravos if they would
undertake to kill me.

"You can still perceive, in spite of my
age, and the troubles that have weighed
me down, that I was agile when a youth,
and that I was capable of taking care of
myself against ten priests. Well, Alba
had come to tell me of her father's death
and the priest's calumnies. And this scoundrel had me waylaid, as she warned me,
so that I ran a narrow escape of losing my
life. He had paid several cut-throats hand-
somely to destroy me. I was always,
however, on my guard, and seldom went
out of the house without my carbine; and
my faithful little dog Lion could hear the
movement of a small bird a hundred paces
off, and would wag his tail and prick up
his ears at the slightest sound. My poor,
poor dog! he was a victim to his love
for me."

And here the sensitive heart of the old chief, Gasparo, obliged him to pause a moment.

"Yes, those devils, during one of my walks to S——, contrived to poison him.

"From S—— to my forest-home several thick places in the cover had to be passed. Here the bravos had hidden themselves once or twice, but, frustrated by my vigilance, and frightened at my carbine, they made their retreat as soon as I appeared, and informed the priest that they should give up the enterprise. Father Giacomo did not understand this, and finally persuaded them, after offering a higher sum, and regaling them abundantly with food and wine, to make another attempt, in which he himself was to accompany them. With his three highwaymen, he took up a position one evening near my little house, all four concealing themselves behind a large bush that grew by the side of the narrow path which led to it, and which they knew I should be obliged to pass.

"My poor Lion was dead, and on this

occasion, in spite of all my precautions, I *was* taken by surprise. Four almost simultaneous shots were fired upon me from the bush, and a furious cry of 'Die' was uttered by the would-be assassins, who rushed upon me expecting to find me mortally wounded. But not so, for I was saved as by a miracle. All four balls struck me, and three of them slightly wounded me, the most serious hurt being caused by the first shot, which carried off, as you see, a piece of my left ear; the second struck against my leathern belt, smashing only a few of my cartridges; the third pierced my hat, grazing my head; and the fourth grazed my right shoulder, occasioning but a slight scratch.

"The first person who approached me was the priest, holding a carbine in his left hand and a poniard in the right. He was like a demon to behold, for rage and hatred; but my shot was more effective than his, and in one moment he was rolling at my feet, uttering frightful groans. I knocked over one of the bravos with my second discharge, whereupon the other two,

seeing the figure their companions had cut,
and noting the pistols still left in my belt,
took to their heels and fled. This was the
first time I had shed blood, and I felt some
remorse as I regarded the dead bodies of
the priest and his tool. In any other
country I might have escaped unpunished
by pleading the law of self-defence; for
though I had no witnesses, the case was
clear, and the rancour which the priest
bore to me was so well known, that it
would not have been difficult to prove my
innocence. But under the priestly government it is another matter, and the destroyer
of one of their body would have no chance
of escape; so I thought it best to flee the
country.

"Then began the eventful history of my
so-called brigandage; and I swear to you
that amongst all the agents sent out of
this world by my hand, there has not been
one who did not first attempt my life.
Many young men, persecuted like me by
the clergy, followed me to my place of
retreat; and very soon I had organised so

formidable a band, that the Papal Government treated with me almost as with an equal power. Assassins or thieves by profession I never would receive into my company. The unfortunate of all grades were aided by me; and if the authorities of the priesthood were sometimes assaulted, it was only to warn them to cease their acts of injustice and infamy.

" In this manner I passed many years, in reality more of a ruler over the Roman country than he who sits in the Quirinal, until the creatures of that cunning court, seeing they could do nothing with me by force, had recourse to treachery. That bright jewel of holiness, my relative, Cardinal A——, whom may God reward! contributed more than any one else to my capture. I had the weakness to trust his specious promises, and remained, in consequence, fourteen years in irons in a miserable prison. But the justice of God will at last find out those evil doers and punish them, for they are verily the scourge of humanity.

"When in the Papal galleys I heard of you, Orazio, and of your courageous resistance to the tools of the Vatican, and I assure you I prayed Heaven that I might become before I died your assistant and companion. My prayer was heard, and I only desire to devote the short remainder of my life to the cause defended by you and your noble comrades."

Julia was interested in the narrative of the famous bandit, and, after sympathising with him, was about to ask Orazio to relate some passages of his career, when, looking around at the company, she perceived from their looks that repose after the fatigues of the day had become necessary ; and, as the hour was late, she abandoned the idea, and watched with curiosity the preparations for sleeping in the open air.

Fresh branches from the trees were strewn upon the most level portions of the ground, under some of the gigantic oaks of the wood, and thus a magnificent sylvan couch was spread apart for the women, who were to rest together, covered with the cloaks of their beloved ones. Muzio offered his to Julia, with a pleading look, and repaid her with a glance of the deepest gratitude when she graciously accepted it. In the meantime Orazio and his friends placed guards and sentinels around, and gave orders to sound the *reveillé* at dawn.

There, under the trees, extended on the turf, slept those upon whom the hopes of all true Romans hung. For Rome, after eighteen centuries of lethargy and shame, was beginning to awake and claim again a place of honour on the earth for her who was once its mistress.

CHAPTER XLIX.

HEAVEN has apparently willed that the highest pitch of human greatness shall be in its turn contrasted with the lowest depths of national humiliation. Witness that body of cut-throats now called the "*Roman army*," compared with the "ROMAN ARMY" which once conquered all the known world. None but priests could have produced such an astounding and monstrous transformation.

While the hours had passed as above related, the General placed at the head of the Pope's troops arrived at Viterbo, with all the forces he had been able to gather, and called his superior officers to a council in the municipal palace. Among the number was one martial gentleman, with a nose like a small melon, covered with slips of sticking-plaster, and this warrior was he

who had received the blow from Silvio at
the inn door.   His face was flushed besides
with wine, of which he had been partaking
copiously to drown his chagrin, and he
urged the General vehemently to proceed
at once to assault the "*brigands.*"   The
General, however, considered that it would
be better to wait till daybreak before they
made a move, for he was by no means
certain that the soldiers could stand to
their arms at that late hour, nearly all
being more or less drunk; and, after some
further discussion, the General's view was
applauded by the council and adopted.

At daybreak, therefore, the champions of
the altar and the tiara obeyed the bugle
call; but it required some little time to
get these ornaments of warfare into order.
Some were footsore by the rapid march
from Rome to Viterbo, others by their
flight from the Ciminian hill, others ill
with potations, and therefore it was not
until the sun rose high above the Apen-
nines that the army was in marching order.
Even then many were the delays, for the

General was at the mercy of the native
guides, who very unwillingly conducted
him through the intricacies of the forest,
of which he was of course ignorant.

The proscribed, who were thoroughly
acquainted with it, had begun to move at
early dawn, so that when the sun rose
they had already reached the summit of
the mountain, from whence they could
survey the whole country, and were reconnoitring, to see if any troops were advancing
from the town. The coming of the troops
was thus directly perceived.

Orazio—whose assumption of the command no one had disputed—dispersed about
a hundred of his men, under Muzio's
direction, as skirmishers over the low lands
and amongst the underwood bordering
upon the road on which the enemy was
advancing. The remainder he arranged in
column on the rising ground, ordering
them to be in readiness to charge at the
first signal. Having thus disposed his
main force, he summoned Captain Tortiglio, and questioned him about the

different officers in command of the enemy, who was still at some distance, ascending the mountain side.

"He who commands the vanguard," replied Tortiglio, "is Major Pompone, a brave officer, but a bully of the first order."

"If I do not deceive myself," said Silvio, who was watching the enemy's movements through his telescope, "that is the very fellow who wanted me to carry his luggage for him, for his nose is unmistakable."

"And who is that on horseback, leading what I suppose to be the principal body?" again asked Orazio.

"Lend me your telescope," said Tortiglio, and, having pointed it at the individual in question, exclaimed, "*Per Dio!* that is the commander-in-chief of the Papal army; and see, his mounted staff is just appearing!"

"What is his name?"

· "His name is Count de la Roche—de la Roche Haricot. These French Legitimists, representatives of the feudal times, have names nearly all commencing with *de*,

which are very difficult for us, 'of the *Si*,'
to pronounce."

" You, then, belong to the language of
the *Si*, Signor Spaniard?" asked Orazio
rather roughly.

" *Come no!* " (and why not?) articulated
the captain in Spanish; "are you alone the
sons of the ancient Latins, and the posses-
sors of that universal language? Learn
that there is as much in common between
the Italian, Spanish, and Portuguese lan-
guages as there is between the face of a
Calabrian and that of an Andalusian, who,
indeed, resemble each other like brothers."

" Bravo, Captain Tortiglio," said Attilio,
who had just arrived, having left the division
he was in command of for orders; "you are
a fortunate scholar! We unlucky Romans
are only taught by the priests to kiss hands,
kneel, and attend the mass, but are left in
ignorance of what goes on in grammars and
polite learning outside the walls of Rome."

But the Papal army was advancing, and
Orazio, like an experienced captain, kept
measuring its progress, without being in the

least discomposed, yet feeling that anxiety which a leader must experience when in command of a body of troops of any kind, and in the presence of a numerous enemy about to attack.

One of the inconveniences a guerilla band has to sustain in time of battle, and which very much pre-occupies the chief, is the necessity of abandoning the wounded in case of retreat, or of leaving them in charge of the terrified inhabitants, who are afraid of being compromised. These considerations, and the unequal number of the opposing forces, impelled Orazio to sound the signal for retiring, and the hunter, with the sagacity that distinguished him, gathered in his fifty men with as much coolness as he would have shown had he been summoning them to a new beat in the chase. Having communicated his intention to Attilio, and enjoined him not to attempt it too precipitately, but to execute the order of retreat in divisions, Orazio went to Muzio, who was prepared to receive the enemy, now marching rapidly upon him.

Exchanging a few words with the leader of the vanguard, he ascended to the highest point of the position, from whence he was able to survey everything, accompanied only by two of his adjutants.

General Haricot was not wanting in a certain amount of gallantry, which would have been worthy of a better cause. He was now assailing the unknown position of the Liberals boldly, with his vanguard *en echelon*, being himself in the centre of the line.

However it may be—whether in a skirmish or in a pitched battle—the commander-in-chief ought to place himself in such a manner that he can command a view of as large a portion of the field of battle as the circumstances permit, and this he can usually best accomplish, by being himself at the head of the troops first engaged.

As he must receive information of all that passes during the fight, the General, if he posts himself at a distance from the scene of action, subjects himself to serious loss of time, inaccurate reports, and, to what is of still greater importance, incapability to dis-

cover at a glance that portion of his command which may stand in immediate want
of relief, or to note where, if victorious,
he ought to send in pursuit of the enemy
light bodies of cavalry, infantry, or artillery,
to complete the repulse.

There was no failing, however, in this
respect on the part of the two commanders-
in-chief in this action.

Haricot, emboldened by the superiority
of his numbers, gave the order to attack without any hesitation. Orazio, though decided
upon a retreat on account of his inferior
force, was determined to give his opponent
such a lesson as should make him more
guarded and less precipitous in his pursuit.

The irregularity of the ground, and the
dense masses of trees had enabled Muzio to
draw his men under cover into advantageous
positions. There he desired them to await
till the enemy came into point-blank range,
to fire only telling shots, and then retreat
behind the lines of the other divisions.

This his valorous companions in arms did.
Their first discharge covered the ground with

the wounded and lifeless bodies of the
enemy. The vanguard of the mercenaries
was so demoralised as to retire, and while
supports, led on by the intrepid chief, were
staying their backward progress, the confusion gave the Italians time to make their
retreat in good order.

When Cortes disembarked at Mexico he
burned his ships. When the Thousand of
Marsala disembarked in Sicily they also
abandoned their vessels to the enemy, and
so deprived themselves of any hope of return; and truly these courageous acts con-
duced much to the success and triumphant
conduct of both expeditions.

The proximity of friendly frontiers has
often been the cause of defection in the
ranks of the patriotic Italians. We have
witnessed such scandals in Lombardy in
1848, caused by the tempting neighbourhood of Switzerland, and also unhappily in
the Roman states by the nearness of the
royal territory.

Such was the case with the Three Hundred.
After the many adventures here related,

Orazio acccomplished his retreat from the Ciminian hill without loss, but it was necessary to retire as far as the Italian dominion, and then it happened with his followers just as might have been expected, from their want of supplies and the temptation of safety.

Although this band was composed of courageous men, it dissolved like a fog before the sun when it touched the national frontier. The chiefs, after vainly reminding their men that their country was still in bondage, and that it was the duty of all to prepare for another struggle to free her, found themselves nearly alone. The eight or nine firm hearts with whom we are best acquainted, along with Gasparo and Jack, followed the road to Tuscany on their way to Leghorn, where they expected to find the fair Julia's yacht, and gain some news of their absent friends. And here we will take leave of them for the present, to meet them later in new and adventurous scenes.

END OF PART I.

PART THE SECOND.

—◆—

CHAPTER L.

THE PILGRIMAGE.

GENERAL GARIBALDI, at the period where we renew our story, was on the mainland, whither he had been called by his friends. He had left his rocky abode to fulfil a duty towards Italy, to which country he had long dedicated his life. He had forced himself to undertake a pilgrimage, setting out from the Venetian territory, his end being not only to influence the political elections, but to sow the germs of emancipated spirit and conscience, which alone can restore Italy to her old state of national greatness, and enable her people to throw off their bonds; discountenancing utterly that idolatrous and false Church called Papal, and living upon

the truths of a real and vital religion. For
with the priests human brotherhood is impossible, since the Papist condemns to ever-
lasting flames every member of the human
family who refuses belief in the Pope's
supremacy. In like manner the Dervish or
Turkish priest condemns eternally every be-
liever in Christianity, and you cannot walk
safely in the streets of Constantinople or
Aleppo because your life is in danger
from these fanatics. In short, priests and
bigots are pretty much alike all over
the world; while the greatest and most
sanguinary of conflicts have always been
fomented by them.

Take as an example the Crimean
war, where one hundred and fifty thousand men perished, while enormous
treasures were swallowed up by the con-
test. The commencement of the quarrel
was on account of the church named the
Holy Sepulchre, and to decide whether a
Papistical or a Greek priest should take
precedence there. This dispute was brought
before the Emperors of France and Russia,

and the result was—war; England and
Italy taking part in the enormous butchery
that followed.

England is at the present day much
troubled with regard to the state of Ireland,
largely caused by the priests; and may God
spare the world from an insurrection in the
United States, where, in a population of
thirty-three millions, nearly half are Roman
Catholics, a large proportion of them being
Irish, who, under the dictatorship of their
bishops, divide the country, and are always
plotting for political supremacy!

In Venice the greater part of the population swore to follow General Garibaldi to
the death, yet the day after the same crowd
congregated in those shops where religious
trinkets and "indulgences" in God's name
are sold for money, and where idolatry in
the guise of Christianity erects vain and
lying images. Such are the Venetians,
and such are they likely to remain under
priestly superstition and political corruption.

With regard to representation, the great

body of the Italian people are excluded
from the elective franchise. Out of a population of more than twenty-five millions
there are only four million five hundred
thousand voters. Every voter must be
twenty-five years of age, and must be
able to read and write. As to the latter,
the power of signing his name is deemed
sufficient, but he must also contribute
an annual sum of not less than forty
francs, which must be paid in direct
taxation to the state or province (the
province answering to the English
county); the municipal rates not being
taken into account. Graduates of uni-
versities, members of learned societies,
military and civil *employés* either upon
active service or half-pay, professional
men, schoolmasters, notaries, solicitors,
druggists, licensed veterinary surgeons,
agents of change, and all persons living
in a house, or having a shop, magazine, or
workshop, are entitled to a vote, provided
the rental is, in communes containing a
population of less than two thousand five

hundred inhabitants, two hundred francs;
and in communes containing a population
of from two thousand five hundred to ten
thousand inhabitants, three hundred francs;
and in communes containing a population of
over ten thousand inhabitants, four hundred
francs. But the power which the Government has of unduly influencing such of the
voters as are not in its own immediate
employ is enormous, by means of the chief
officer in every town, called the syndic,
who is appointed by the Government, and
removable at its pleasure.

This officer, under pain of dismissal,
recommends to the voters for election any
candidate that the Government desires to
have elected, and lamentable as is the
financial state of the country, millions of
francs were placed at the disposal of the
syndics for the purpose of corruption in
the spring of the year 1867. If a town
wants a branch railway to the main line,
the election of the Government candidate
will always insure the accomplishment of its
wishes on this point.

The whole host of Government officials, including the police, actively interfere in aid of the ministerial candidate. School-masters and others will be dismissed from their posts if they give a refractory vote; and workmen for the same reason are dis-charged. Official addresses have been known to be openly published, desiring the people not to vote for the opposition candi-dates; and there are instances of papers on the day of election being withheld from those voters who might prove to be too independent.

Therefore, it was with a view to reform-ing these abuses that General Garibaldi, in addressing the municipality of Palma, said, "Let the new Chambers be impressed with the necessity of reorganising the ad-ministration, and if the Government, to tempt them, returns to its evil ways, then ill betide it."

We do not intend following the General's steps as he proceeded from town to town, enthusiastically received by the multitude, who, joyous at the sight of the "man of

the people," applauded his doctrine of
non-submission to foreign dominion and
humiliation, and above all echoed his plain
denunciations of clerical infamy and that
immoral understanding which exists between
the Papacy and those unworthy men who
misgovern Italy.

As may be supposed, the priests attacked the General, and accused him far
and wide of being an atheist. This false
and foolish charge led to his delivering the
following address before twenty thousand
people at Padua :—

. "It is in vain that my enemies try to
make me out an atheist. I believe in God.
I am of the religion of Christ, not of the
religion of the Popes. I do not admit any
intermediary between God and man. Priests
have merely thrust themselves in, in order
to make a trade of religion. They are the
enemies of true religion, liberty, and progress ; they are the original cause of our
slavery and degradation, and in order to
subjugate the souls of Italians, they have
called in foreigners to enchain their bodies.

The foreigners we have expelled, now we must expel those mitred and tonsured traitors who summoned them. The people must be taught that it is not enough to have a free country, but that they must learn to exercise the rights and perform the duties of free men. Duty! duty! that is the word. Our people must learn their duties to their families, their duties to their country, their duties to humanity."

Garibaldi proceeded next to the university of Padua; and there, standing before the statue of Galileo, he uncovered his head, saying, "Who, remembering Galileo, his genius and his life, the torture inflicted upon him, the martyrdom he suffered—he, I say, who, remembering this, does not despise the priests of Rome, is not worthy to be called a man or an Italian."

The interests of commerce having always had a place in the heart of General Garibaldi, he delivered the following address to the Representatives of the Chambers of Commerce for Vicenza:—"Italy's future depends in great part on you. Our wars

against the foreigners are, I hope, nearly at
an end. Italy is united, is independent;
you can make her prosperous. There is
nothing necessary to the maintenance of
the human race that we cannot produce;
and with such raw material as we have,
what can we not manufacture? Our people
have a mania for foreign goods; they like
to wear foreign stuffs, to drink foreign
wines; but let them once be persuaded that
our own are as good, and they will be glad
to adopt them; and foreign nations will
receive our merchandise, our manufactures,
as eagerly as we now seek for theirs. But
progress of every kind is difficult with the
priests, and human brotherhood impossible."

CHAPTER LI.

THE MEMORY OF THE DEAD.

LET our tale revert to yet more distant memories, while the name of "Italy" wakes the author's recollections. He is set thinking of the sad times when newly-liberated Rome was again enchained by the hands of European despotism, alarmed at the revival of the Mistress of the World, and at the terrible warning conveyed by the Roman Republic. Alas! it was by the arms of another great Republic that her hopes were blighted. Napoleon, the secret enemy of all liberty, fleshed his weapons upon the Romans when he had committed the crime of *lesa-nazione*, and betrayed the credulous people of Paris, slaying them in their streets without regard to age or sex. May God, in his own time, deal with the assassin of the 2nd of December, and of the world's liberty !

After the defence of Rome, the General, never despairing of the fate of Italy, although left with but few followers, decided to take the field. But more is required than a handful of brave men when nations intend to liberate themselves; and what can an irregular band of intrepid youths accomplish against four armies?

It is true that in the present day national spirit is more awakened, and the handful of brave youths has grown to heroic proportions and historical deeds; but in those unhappy times the populace stood gazing stupefied and in silence at the relics of the defenders of Rome while passing out on their way to the open country, regarding them as irretrievably lost. Not one of those cowards stood forward to increase our ranks. On the contrary, every morning discovered a quantity of arms upon the ground of bivouac, which deserters had abandoned. Those arms were placed upon the mules and wagons

which accompanied the column, so that
in time the column possessed more mules
and wagons than men, and little by little
the hope of arousing that nation of slug-
gards vanished from the souls of the faithful
and courageous survivors.

At San Marino, seeing there was no
longer any hope or heart to fight, the
order of the day was given "to dismiss
the men to their homes." That order
was couched in the following terms: "Return to your homes, but remember that
Italy must not remain a slave."

The larger number took the road to
their dwellings, but some deserters from
the Papal and Austrian troops, who, if
taken prisoner would have been shot, remained to accompany their chief in his
last attempt to free Venice.

And here begins a still sadder and
more painful history.

Anita, the General's inseparable companion, would not, even under these
trying circumstances, leave him. In vain
did her husband endeavour to persuade

her to remain at San Marino. Though pregnant, faint, and sick, arguments were of no avail : the courageous woman would heed no advice, and answered all by smilingly asking "if he wished to abandon her."

Surrounded by the Austrian troops, tracked by the Papal police, that tired remnant of the Roman army outstripped them all during a night march, and arrived at the gates of Cesenatico at one o'clock in the morning, where an Austrian detachment kept guard.

"Fall on them and disarm them," exclaimed Garibaldi to the few individuals forming his retinue; and the Austrian soldiers, completely stupefied, allowed themselves to be disarmed.

The authorities were then awakened, and requested to supply food and small barges, that the volunteers might embark.

It cannot be denied that fortune has favoured the General in many arduous enterprises, but at this time began for him a series of adversities and misfortunes.

A northern cloud had spread itself over the Adriatic on this night, and breaking into wind, had rendered the sea furious. The narrow mouth of the port of Cesenatico was one mass of foam. Great were the efforts made to leave the port in the barges, thirteen in number, weighed down as they were with people, and at day-break they succeeded—but at this crisis numerous Austrians entered the place.

Sail was made, for the wind had become favourable, and on the following morning four of the barges, in one of which were Garibaldi and Anita, with Ciceruachio, his two sons, and Ugo-Bassi, landed in the Foci del Po. Anita, carried in the arms cf the man of her heart, was borne to shore in a dying condition.

The occupants of the other nine barges had given themselves up to the Austrian squadron, which had discovered the little crafts by the light of a full moon, and had rained bullets and grape-shot upon them until they surrendered.

The shores where the four boats put in were swarming with the enemy's explorers, sent to trace the fugitives.

Anita was lying a little way off the shore, concealed in a corn-field, her head supported by her husband. Leggiero, a valiant major belonging to the island of Maddalena, who had followed the General in South America, and returned to Italy with him, was their only companion. He lay peeping through the stalks, and very soon discovered some of the cursed white curs in search of blood.

Ciceruachio, Bassi, and nine others, who by our advice had taken a different direction in order to escape the enemy, were all captured, and shot like dogs by the Austrians.

When the nine companions were taken, the Austrians compelled nine peasants, by force of blows, to dig nine holes in the sand, after which a discharge from the enemy's picket dispatched the unhappy heroes. The youngest, a son of a Roman Tribune, only thirteen years of age, still moved after the fire, but a blow from the

H 2

butt-end of an Austrian's musket smashed
in his skull, and thus brutally ended his
young life.

Bassi and his brother, Ciceruachio, met
with the same fate at Bologna.

The foreigner and the priest made merry
in that hour of slaughter over the purest
Italian blood; and the mitred master of
Rome remounted his polluted throne,
having for a footstool the corpses of his
compatriots.

Let this cold brutality, this savage
butchery of their honest noble-hearted
champions live in the memory of Italians,
and give their consciences no peace while
they leave their magnificent city a prey
to the foreigner and to the vile priests,
who use it as a den of infamy.

The General, bearing his precious burden—that dear and faithful wife—wandered sadly, with his companion, Leggiero,
through the lagoons of the lower Po,
until he had closed her eyes, and wept
over her cold corpse tears of desperation.
Onwards he wandered then, through

forests and over mountains, ever pursued by the agents of the Pope and of Austria.

Fate, however, spared him, to suffer anew both danger and fatigue, and to reap some triumphs too.

The tyrants of Italy again found him upon their tracks—those tracks indelibly stained by them with tears and blood. Ill was it for them that he had escaped until that day when they, in turn, took to flight, and like cowards, left their tables spread for him, while the carpets of their superb palaces bore the imprint of the rough shoes of his Thousand.

Meanwhile, however, our tale has brought the General to Venice to witness the liberty for which he had sighed so much. It was then that the lagunes covered with gondolas, saluted the *Red Shirt* as the token of national redemption, and sad memories faded in the light of the joy and freedom of that Queen of the Adriatic.

CHAPTER LII.

IT is eleven o'clock at night. The canals
of Venice are covered with gondolas, and
the Place of St. Mark, illuminated, is so
crowded with people that scarcely a stone
of the pavement is visible.

From the balcony of the Zecchini Palace,
on the north side of the Piazza, the General
has saluted the people and the redeemed
city—"redeemed," yes, but by a bargain
—the ancient bulwark of European civilisation was, alas! bought and *sold* a bargain
between courts—and that salutation was
frantically responded to by an exulting and
affected multitude.

And above all was the beholder struck
by the aspect of the populace, as he said
to himself, "The stigma which despotism
imprints upon the human face can even
be discerned here.

" A people, once the ancient rulers of the world, is transformed by the foreigner and the priest, whose rod of deception, dipped in the chemistry of superstition, is able to change good into evil, gold to dross, and the most prosperous of nations into one of beggars and sacristans. These have bartered for their noble city of the sea, which calls herself ' daughter of Rome '—left her disheartened, dishonoured, and defamed!" And he who loved the people cried out in the anguish of his soul, "Alas, that it should be so!"

But moved as he was by the contemplation of the scene, he did not, nevertheless, fail to cast a scrutinising look over the buzzing crowd. After a life of sixty years, into which so many events had been crowded, the man of the people was not wanting in the experience that enabled him to analyse fairly the component parts of a densely-packed crowd, among whom were hidden the thief, the assassin, the spy, and the hireling of the priest. And many such were purposely mingled with the good and honest of that population.

While thoughtfully gazing, as we have said, upon the assembled people, a slight touch upon his shoulder made him aware of Attilio's presence.

"Do you see," said the young Roman to him, "that scoundrel's face, whose head is covered with a cap of the Venetian fashion, standing amongst those simple Venetian souls, but as easy to be distinguished as a viper amongst lizards, or a venomous tarantula amongst ants? When such reptiles wind about in a crowd, it is not without a motive; he is sent from Rome, and there is certainly something new in store for us. That fellow is Cencio. I must look to him a little!"

Our readers will remember the subaltern agent of Cardinal Procorpio, for whom Gianni had rented a room in sight of Manlio's studio. After his employers had been hanged, he had been promoted to a higher office, that of principal agent to his Eminence Cardinal ——, the Pope's prime minister.

Cencio, once a liberal, afterwards a traitor,

had made profitable use of his knowledge of some of the democrats of Rome, and was, therefore, prized as a secret agent by the Cardinal's tribunal.

We shall presently see what his mission to Venice had been. Meantime, in a saloon in the Zecchini Palace, closely filled with guests, amongst the brightest of the Venetian beauties shone our three heroines, Irene, Julia, and Clelia.

The Venetian youths, accustomed to contemplate the charms of the daughters of the Queen of the Adriatic, were nevertheless astounded at the enchanting appearance of these three Roman ladies. We say three Romans, because Julia had by this time espoused her Muzio, and, although an affectionate daughter of her own dear native land, she was proud of her adopted country, and called herself a Roman.

Irene was a little older than her companions, but had preserved so much freshness, that her extremely majestic carriage covered the difference of years, and she had so much the perfection of womanhood about

her, that she could well have served as a
model to an artist wishing to portray one
of those grand Roman matrons of Cornelia's
time.

Marriage had not changed her younger
and equally lovely companion; and the trio
formed such an ornament to that drawing-
room that the Venetian youths fluttered
around them perfectly dazzled and amazed.
By the side of Clelia were Manlio and
the gentle Silvia. Of all our ladies only
the Signora Aurelia was missing, and she
had ended her unintentionally adventurous
career by marrying the good-natured Captain
Thompson, to whom she clung like the ivy
to the oak; and although the sea was still
a little repugnant to her, on account of that
storm in which she had suffered so much,
yet the billows had lost much of their terror
now that her British sea-lion was by her
side to guard her.

Orazio and Muzio were standing together
in a corner of the room talking over the
events of the day, when Attilio, going up
to them, made them acquainted with his

discovery, and after some consultation they started off in company to the Piazza di San Marco.

Not a few vain efforts did the three friends make to break through the crowd before they succeeded in at last reaching the object of their search, and whilst General Garibaldi, recalled by the people to the balcony, was again addressing the crowd, he saw his three young friends surround the fictitious Venetian.

The iron hand of Orazio grasped the wrist of the agent like a vice, and Muzio, whose voice the scoundrel had formerly heard, fixing his glittering eyes upon him, said in a low tone, "Cencio, come with us." The tool of the priests, the traitor of the meeting at the Baths of Caracalla, trembled from head to foot, his florid face became pale as that of a corpse, and, without articulating a word, he walked forward in the direction indicated by Muzio, between the other two Romans, who pushed him unresistingly on.

CHAPTER LIII.

THE "GOVERNMENT."

WHEN one thinks upon the hardly accomplished union of this our Italy, and of the rulers who have "led" her over the thorny path she has trodden, one cannot but bow before the wisdom of Providence, who has uplifted her until she has constituted herself a nation.

Often in meditating upon this—our beautiful, grand, but unhappy native land—we in imagination have pictured her as a chariot drawn with patient toil by the generous portion of the people, having for device the "good of all," preceded by the star of Providence like a shining beacon, with the wicked host of rulers and their immense retinue following behind, disconcerted and fatigued, holding on to and endeavouring to draw back the vehicle of the state, even at the risk of destroying it in their efforts; while the people, impoverished, checked, and humiliated by that heavy treason tugging in the rear, remain submissive and constant in their labours, clearing away the obstacles that cross their path towards redemption, and proceeding gradually forward without despairing of a future reparation. Reparation, indeed! From whom, my countrymen, do you expect reparation? From the re-assured professors of priestcraft, of Jesuitism, and of imposture, who have been restored to your towns and villages at the expense of your patrimony to maintain you in ignorance and in misery?

One of the many means of corruption employed by the powerful to render the populace slaves, is at the present day the " black division "—the priests. Kings who no longer believe in them have begun to use them to control the people, and keep them from justice, light, and liberty, in the name of " religion." This is the " reparation " which thou awaitest, *popolo infelice !* Reparation—and how shouldst thou demand or deserve it, who kneelest daily and hourly at the feet of a lying and chuckling priesthood?

In the meantime, however, one of the agents of this priesthood is walking, with his wicked head held down, in the grasp of Orazio and Attilio; Muzio going before to open the way through the multitude of people, and thus the four arrived finally at a tavern in the Vicola dei Schiavoni.

CHAPTER LIV.

" LET us pass quickly and on tiptoe that
mass of corruption and slaughter called the
Papacy," says Guerrazzi ; or, to quote his
own indignant Italian—

" Passiamo presto, e sulla punta dei
piedi, quel macchio di fimo e di sangue
che si chiama Papato."

The Popes, who call themselves the
vicegerents of Christ, slaughter men with
Chassepôts, play the executioner upon their
political enemies, and instruct the world
in the science of tortures, Inquisitions,
autos-da-fé, and murder. In former days
many unhappy nations had the misfortune
to suffer therefrom. Spain, for example,
who has recently thrown off the yoke, for
centuries groaned under the tortures of
Rome. Even now the priest of Christ in

the Vatican satiates his sanguinary vengeance in various ways, having recourse to
the dagger, poison, brigandage, and murders
of all kinds and degrees.

In the Roman tribunal the sentence of
death had been long pronounced against
Prince T——, the brother of our Irene ;
and Cencio, with eight cut-throats of the
Holy See under his command, was under
orders to take advantage of the tumult
arising upon the arrival of Garibaldi in
Venice to execute the atrocious decree.
The eight accomplices of the spy had been
posted in the immediate neighbourhood of
the Hôtel Victoria, in all the ways by which
he could possibly arrive. Four were to hire
a gondola and ply at the steps, with secret
instructions to despatch the gondoliers if
necessary, that there might be no witness
to lay the charge against them.

Cencio had not undertaken to perform
the actual deed, but simply the task of
following the Prince's movements. Fortunately for the Roman noble the spy
failed in his scent, and was now not only

in the clutches of our three friends who had captured him, but in those of a fourth personage, who was still more formidable to him—no other, in fact, than our old acquaintance Gasparo.

Gasparo, after the events narrated in the preceding chapters, had accompanied his new friends to territory that was not Papal, and had offered his services as attendant to Prince T——. He had therefore accompanied him to Venice. Whilst his master roamed through the saloons of the Zecchini Palace, the watchful follower, who had remained on the threshold to enjoy the sight of that brilliant scene, saw the three Romans whom he loved as sons penetrate into the crowd. He determined to keep near them, and found himself shortly after in the tavern of Vicola dei Schiavoni, at the heels of Cencio.

It would be no easy matter to describe the terror and confusion of the clerical Sinon surrounded by our four friends. They led him to an out-of-the-way room

on the upper storey, and desired the waiter
to bring them something to drink, and then
leave them, as they had some business to
transact.

When the waiter had obeyed them, and
departed, they locked the door, and ordering
the agent to sit against the wall, they
moved to the end of the table, and, seat-
ing themselves upon a bench, placed their
elbows on the table and fixed a look upon
the knavish wretch which made him tremble.

Under any other circumstances the
wretch would have inspired compassion,
and might have been forgiven for his
treachery, in consideration of his present
agony of fear.

The four friends, cold, impassive, and
relentless, satisfied themselves for some
time with fixing their eyes upon the
traitor, while he, quite beside himself,
with wide-opened mouth and eyes, was
doing his best to articulate something;
but all he could mutter was, " Signore—I
—am—not," and other less intelligible
monosyllables.

The calmness of the four Romans was somewhat savage, but for their deep cause of hatred; and if any one could have contemplated the scene he would have been reminded forcibly of the fable of the rat under the inexorable gaze of the terrier-dog, which watches every movement, and then pounces out upon it, crunching all the vermin's bones between its teeth. Or could a painter have witnessed that silent assembly, he would have found a subject for a striking picture of deep-seated wrath and abject terror.

We have already described the persons of the three friends—true types of the ancient Roman—with fine and artistic forms. Gasparo was even more typical—one of those heads which a French photographist would have delighted to " take " as the model of an Italian brigand—and the picture would have been more profitable than the likeness of any European sovereign. He was indeed, in his old age, a superb image of a brigand, but a brigand of the nobler sort. One of those who hate with a deadly hatred the cut-throat rabble; one that never stained himself with any covetous or infamous action, as the paid miscreants of the priests do, who commit acts that would fill even a panther's heart with horror.

Even the successor of Gianni would have made a valuable appearance in a *quadro caratteristico*, for certainly no subject could have served better to display panic in all its disgusting repulsiveness. Glued to the wall behind him, he would, if his strength had equalled his wish, have knocked it down, or, bored his way through it to get further from those four terrible countenances, which stared impassively and mercilessly at him, meditating upon his ruin, perhaps upon his death.

The austere voice of Muzio, already described as the chief of the Roman *contropolizia*, was the first to break that painful silence.

"Well, then, Cencio," he began, "I will tell you a story which, as you are a Roman,

you may perhaps know, but, at all events,
you shall know it now.

"One day our forefathers, tired of the rule
of the first king of Rome—who, amongst
other amiable things, had killed his brother
Remus with a blow because he amused
himself with jumping over the walls he
had erected around Rome—our fathers, I
repeat, by a *senatus consultum*, decided to
get rid of their king, who was rather too
meddlesome and despotic. *Detto-fatto!*
they rushed upon him with their daggers,
and, although he struggled valorously,
Romulus fell under their blows. But now
the deed was done, it was necessary to invent
a stratagem, for the Roman people were
somewhat partial to their warlike king.
They accordingly accepted the advice of
an old senator, who said, 'We will tell
the people that Mars (the father of
Romulus) has descended amongst us, and,
after reproaching us for thieving a little too
much, and being indignant to see the son
of a god at our head, has carried him off
to heaven.'

" 'But what are we to do with the body?' asked several of the senators.

" 'With the body,' repeated the old man ; ' nothing is easier.' And drawing forth his dagger, he commenced cutting the corpse in pieces. When this dissection was finished, he said, ' Let each of you take one of these pieces, hide it under your robe, and then go and throw it into the Tiber. It is evening now, and by to-morrow morning the sea-monsters will have given a decent burial to the founder of Rome.'"

" Now Cencio, don't you think that, as regards your own end, and not being king of Rome, or son of a god, such a death would be very honourable to you who are nothing more than a miserable traitor?"

" For God's sake," screamed the terrified agent, trembling like a child, " I will do whatever you demand of me; but, for the love you bear your friends, your wives, your mothers, do not put me to such a cruel death."

" Do you talk of a cruel death? Can

there be a death too cruel for a spy—a traitor?" asked Muzio. "Have you already forgotten," he continued, "vile reptile, selling the Roman youths to the priests at the Baths of Caracalla; and that they narrowly escaped being slaughtered by your infamy?"

Tears continued to roll from the coward's eyes, as Muzio continued: "What about your arrival in Venice? What does it mean? Who sent you? What did you come here for, dog?"

"I will tell all," was the wretched man's reply.

"You had better tell all," repeated Muzio, "or we shall see with edge of knife whether you have concealed anything in that malicious and treacherous carcase of yours."

"All, all!" cried Cencio like a maniac; and, as if forgetful of what he had to relate, or overpowered by great fright, he appeared not to know how or where to begin.

"You are doubtless more prompt in your

narration to the Holy Office, stammerer,"
grumbled Gasparo.

"Begin!" shouted Orazio; and Attilio,
in a stern voice, also cried "Begin!" not
having spoken until then.

A moment of death-like silence followed
before Cencio commenced thus:—

"If the life of Prince T—— is dear to
you——"

"Prince T——, the brother of Irene,"
exclaimed Orazio, clearing the table at one
bound, and grasping the traitor by the
throat.

Had Cencio been clutched in the claws
of a tiger, he would not have felt more
helpless than he did now, held by the fingers
of the "Prince of the Roman campagna."

Attilio said gently, "Brother, have
patience—let him speak; if you choke him
we shall gain no information."

The suggestion made by the chief of the
Three Hundred seemed reasonable to Orazio,
and he withdrew his impatient grip from
Cencio's throat.

"If the life of Prince T—— is dear to

you," again recommenced the knave, "let us go all together in search of him, and inform him that eight emissaries of the Holy Office are lurking about the Hôtel Victoria, where he is lodging, in order to assassinate him."

CHAPTER LV.

DEATH TO THE PRIESTS.

" DEATH to the priests!" shouted the people.

"*Death to no one!*" replied the General to the crowd from the balcony, in answer to their cry.

"*Death to no one!* Yet none are worthier of death than this villainous sect, which for private ends, disguised as religious, has made Italy 'the land of the dead,' a burial-ground of greatness! Beccaria, thy doctrines are true and right! The shedding of blood is impious. But I know not if Italy will ever be able to free herself from those who tyrannise over her soul and body without annihilating them with the sword for pruning-hook, even to the last branch!"

These reflections passed through the mind

of the man of the people, although he
rebuked the populace. Meanwhile, those
of them who had not heard the words
uttered by Garibaldi from the balcony,
but only the cry of "Death!" which thou-
sands of excited voices had re-echoed—
those of the people, we repeat, who were
furthest off from the General and near
the palace of the Patriarch, advanced like
the flood of a torrent precipitating itself
from a mountain, and attacked the prelate's
abode, overturning all obstacles opposed
to their fury. In a few minutes every
saloon, every room in this fine building
was invaded, and through the windows all
those religious idols with which the priests
so unblushingly deceive the people were
seen flying in all directions.

Many artists and lovers of the beautiful
would have lamented and cried, "Scandal!
sacrilege!" at the destruction of such works
of art.

And truly, many very rare and precious
masterpieces, under the form of saint or
Madonna or Bambino, were broken to

pieces and utterly ruined in this work of destruction.

Amongst the cunning acts of the priest-hood—wealthy as they have been made by the stupidity of the "faithful"—has ever been that of employing the most illustrious artists to portray and dignify their legends.

Hence the Michael Angelos and the Raphaels of all periods were lavishly sup-ported by them, and the people, who might have become persuaded of the foolishness of their credulity, and of the impostures of these new soothsayers of Rome, continued to respect the idols of their tyrants by reason of Italian instincts, because these were masterpieces of noble work.

But is not the first masterpiece of a people liberty and national dignity?

And all those wonders of art, although wonders, if they perpetuate with an evil charm our servility, our degradation, oh! would it not be better for them to be sent to the infernal regions!

However, be they precious or worthless works, the people were overturning them and throwing them out upon the pavement that night.

And the Patriarch? Woe to him if he had fallen into the hands of the enraged multitude!

But their sacred skin is dear to those descendants of the apostles! Champions of the faith they may be, but not martyrs.

Of martyrdom the rosy-faced prelates wish to know nothing themselves, if they can avoid it. His Eminence, at the first outbreak of popular indignation, had vanished, gaining, by a secret door, one of his gondolas, in which he escaped in safety.

In the meantime, the cry of the Recluse, "*Morte a nessuno!*" was taken up by the crowd, and at last reached the ears of the sackers of the Patriarch's palace.

That voice, ever trusted and respected by the people, calmed the anger of the passionate multitude, and in a few moments order and tranquillity were again re-established.

CHAPTER LVI.

In the shameful times when the right of the "coscia" existed, princes had little necessity to woo a humble maiden, or to sue for her favour. At the present day things have assumed a different aspect. Although princes exist who possess as much pride of birth, or even more, than those of olden times, still we see many obliged to conform to more moderate pretensions in matters of the heart, aspiring humbly to the favour of a plebeian divinity. Such were the thoughts of poor Prince T——.

He stood in the vestibule of the Zecchini Palace, admiring the throng of graceful visitors.

In the crowded saloons it was difficult to do justice to the faces, and still less to the deportment, of the ladies. From that part

of the vestibule, on the first step, where the
Roman prince had established himself, obser-
vation was easier. Suddenly, from the midst
of the crowd emerged, as if by destiny, one
of those forms which, once seen, are reflected
in the soul for ever. Golden-brown hair,
eyes, and eyelashes, adorned a face which
would have served Titian as a model of
beauty—in a word, he saw the type of the
Venetian ideal.

The Prince, until then immovable in the
crowd hurrying to and fro, was struck by
a glance of those wonderful eyes, which
seemed to look at everything and everybody,
without for a moment fixing their glance
on any.

As if under a spell, the Prince rushed
after the footsteps of the unknown lady,
whose light form seemed to float over the
ground. He hurried on after her, but the
wish to overtake her was one thing, the
capability another. The beautiful and graceful girl, either more active or more accustomed to fashionable throngs in Venice, was
already seated in a gondola, and had ordered

the gondolier to put off when the Prince
reached the edge of the canal.

What could he do? throw himself into
the water, and seize on the gunwale of the
lady's boat, like a madman, begging a word
for pity's sake? This was his first impulse;
yet a bath in the waters of the lagoon in
March would be no joke; while to present
himself before the lady of his quest in
the condition which would result from im-
mersion, would be unpropitious, and an
especial trial to the dignity of a man of
rank. He decided on taking a more rational
course, that of embarking in a gondola and
following the incognita.

" Row hard," said the Prince to the
gondolier, " and if you overtake that black
gondola I will reward you well."

Having pointed out the boat to be pursued, the gondolier cried "Avanti" to his
companion at the prow, and turning up his
red shirt sleeves (red shirts being the pre-
vailing fashion just then among the Venetian
rowers, in honour of the guest of the day),
the gondolier prepared to use the oar, with

that grace and vigour which is not to be rivalled by any boatmen in the world.

"Onward! onward! *gondola mia!* onward and overtake that too swift boat, which bears away my life. And why should not that lovely girl be such to me, the Adriatic beauty of which I have dreamed a thousand times, when Venice was enslaved as my poor Rome still is? Yet, why did I only catch a glimpse of her? Why did her dazzling eye thus meet mine, subdue me in a moment, and make me hers for ever, only to disappear? and has not her magic glance wounded others as well as me? The very atmosphere around her intoxicated me; must it not have affected all near her? *Ah, Dio!* is this love at last? Is this that transient passion which men enjoy as they bite at doubtful fruits and throw them away when tasted? or is it that spiritual love which brings the creature near to God, which transforms the miseries of life, its dangers, death itself, into ineffable happiness? Yes! it is that, and now come, ye powerful of the earth! dare but to touch my mistress, whom I love with indescribable

passion, approach her with an army of ruffians at your back, profane but the hem of
her gown, and my sword shall defy all for
her sweet sake!"

"Onward! onward!" cried the Prince,
interrupting his own soliloquy. "Row hard,
my gondolier, and if one crown be not
enough, you shall have ten. Onward!"

"But suppose she were a plebeian?
Well! in the name of heaven what is a
plebeian?

"When God created man, did he make
patricians and plebeians?

"Does not the power that awes the vulgar
come from tyrants and despots?

"Ah! if that beautiful young creature
should prove an impure, a nameless one!

"Oh, blasphemer of love, cease your
profanity! How could a guilty woman's
face show such pure and transcendant love-
liness!"

Anita *was* a plebeian. The entrance to
her dwelling showed that. There stood no
columned porch where the gondola drew
up before a simple door-step. The plain

little staircase was bare; no rich vases with exotic flowers stood about the threshold. A few flower-pots adorned the window-sills, for Anita loved flowers as well as a princess could love them, but hers were little, simple blossoms—I will not say poor ones, for they were dear to the young girl, a very treasure to her.

An aged lady, who by day would have attracted the attention of every one—so great was the anxiety depicted in her face—had awaited until that moment—eleven at night —her beloved girl, who, with the curiosity of a child, had desired, like others, to have a close view of the man of the people. Mario, her only brother, being absent, the mother had confided her to the care of the family gondolier.

When Monna Rosa had ascertained that the newly arrived gondola was that which she expected, she left the balcony, where she had been watching with great misgivings for its arrival, and rapidly descended the stairs, lantern in hand, to receive her beloved child.

The two women were clasped in each other's arms, as if after a long separation, when the Prince arrived, and taking advantage of the open door, and of the engrossed attention of the mother and daughter, he entered the house with the audacity of a soldier on a conquered territory.

At length, disengaged from each other's arms, the mother was exclaiming in a tone of gentle reproach, "Why so late, Anita?" when both started on perceiving the presence of a stranger.

Having entered on a bold adventure, the Prince felt that he must carry it through with spirit. He therefore advanced towards the young girl, who, when so near, seemed more beautiful than ever. He was about to try to find words to excuse his impetuous and irrepressible admiration, when at that moment an iron grasp from behind seized his wrist, and with a shake that made him stagger, separated him from the women.

From a third gondola, which had arrived a short time after the two first, there had sprang out swiftly and resolutely a new and youthful actor on this interesting scene.

Tall in stature, vigorous and handsome in person, the last arrival wore the red shirt, and on the left side of his broad breast bore that distinctive mark of the brave, " The Medal of the Thousand."

Morosini was Anita's lover. An attentive observer would have read in the young girl's face a world of affectionate emotion at the sight of her beloved, succeeded by an expression of affright, when his manly, sonorous voice, addressed the Prince, " You are mistaken, sir! You will not find here the game you seek; retrace your steps, and make your search elsewhere."

The shaking he had received, and the rough words that followed, had roused the Prince's ire, and as he was not wanting in courage, he answered his interlocutor in the same tone.

" Insolent rascal! I came not here to affront, but to offer respectful homage. As for your impertinence, if you are a man of Rome, you will give me satisfaction. Here is my card. I shall be found at the Victoria Hotel, and at your service, until mid-day to-morrow."

"I will not keep you waiting," was Morosini's reply, and with this the disconcerted Prince hurried away.

CHAPTER LVII.

THE Italian sportsman does not pursue the partridge in the thicket; but, after covering up the waters of all the small pools save one, he there awaits his sport with shot, with net, or with bird-lime, at the moment that the innocent creature seeks refuge and refreshment. It is during the sultry hours that the ploughman lies in wait at the watering place, to restore his rebel oxen to the yoke from which they have escaped. The corsair, who would be in vain sought on the ocean, is trapped at the mouth of his hiding place, to which he conducts his prey.

Such was the reasoning of our four Romans as regards Prince T——, for whom they vainly sought in every hole and corner. After they had discovered and sent home the cut-throats of the Holy Office, through the forced assistance of Cencio, they placed themselves on the look-out, in the vicinity of the Victoria Hotel, awaiting the appearance of T——.

In fact, about twelve o'clock, he made his appearance, and was followed to his room by his friends, who made him acquainted with the design of the assassin, and other circumstances.

The Prince was too reserved to inform his friends of his approaching duel, especially Orazio, whose ardent nature he well knew, and who would not have yielded to any other the office of second; still he needed a second, and taking advantage of a moment's animated discussion among his companions, he summoned Attilio to the balcony by a glance, and asked him to remain with him for that night.

Orazio, Muzio, and Gasparo finally took leave, and Attilio remained, under pretext of particular business.

At the first dawn of day, a young man in a red shirt knocked at the door of a room marked No. 8 in the Victoria Hotel, and

presented to Prince T—— a cartel, signed
Morosini, and thus worded :—

" I accept your challenge, and await you
at the door of your hotel in my gondola.
I have weapons with me, but you had better
bring your own, in case mine should not be
suitable. The seconds will regulate the conditions of the duel.
" Morosini."

After the Prince had risen, and summoned Attilio, he introduced him to the
second of Morosini, and in a few minutes
the conditions were settled as to arms,
which were to be pistols ; distance, twenty
steps, to be walked over, firing à volonté.
The ground chosen was behind the Murazzi,
to which the combatants could immediately
repair.

And truly, when one has to die, or to
kill, it is best over as soon as possible, because even the stoutest hearts are disinclined
to either alternative, and wish the time of
expectancy abridged.

What shall I say of duelling ? I have

always thought it disgraceful that men
cannot come to an understanding without
killing one another. But, on the other
hand, it is not time for us, who are still
oppressed by the powerful of the earth,
still the despised of Europe, to preach individual or general peace, to advocate the
forgiveness of private outrages, when we
are often so publicly outraged. We, who
are trampled upon in our rights, our consciences, our honour, by the vilest section
of our nation—we, who, in order to be
allowed life, consideration, and protection,
are compelled to debase ourselves, must not
quite despoil ourselves of our one protection !

Away with duelling, then, when we
shall have a constitution, a well-organised
government — when we shall enjoy our
rights within as well as without; but, in
the present dangerous times for honour and
right, we cannot always proclaim peace.

Meanwhile, the gondolas carrying the
combatants proceeded towards the Murazzi,
the rowers for some time coasting the im-

mense rampart constructed by the Venetian republic as a defence against the fury of the Adriatic, and finally disembarking their passengers on the deserted shore, which is dry when the north winds or the sciroccos blow.

The antagonists leapt on the sand, chose a convenient place, and, after having measured twenty steps, the seconds handed the pistols to the principals, who placed themselves on the two spots marked on the sand. Attilio had to clap his hands three times, and at the third signal the combatants were to walk forward and fire. Already two signals were given; Attilio's hands were again raised to make the third, when a voice cried, from the spot where the gondolas awaited, "Hold!"

The four men all turned in that direction, and saw one of the gondoliers, a venerable, grey-haired man, who was advancing towards them.

"Hold!" repeated the old man; and he came forward without stopping until he stood between the two antagonists. Then he spoke, with a somewhat faltering voice, yet still in a manly tone, with such force as could hardly have been expected in one of his breeding and age—

"Hold! sons of one mother! The act you are about to accomplish will stain one of you with the blood of a compatriot— blood which might flow for the welfare of this unhappy land, which has still so much to do ere she can attain the independence she has aimed at for so many centuries. The vanquished will pass away without one word of love or blessing from those dear to him; the victor will remain for life with the sting of remorse in his heart. You, by whose bronzed and noble face I recognise a child of this unhappy land, has not Italy still many enemies? does she not need all her offspring to loosen the chains of centuries? Abandon, then, this fratricidal struggle, I beseech you, in the name of our common mother! Why should you gratify the enemies of Italy by the murder of her friends? You came forth antagonists, return companions and brothers!"

The waves of the Adriatic were breaking with more effect against the rocks that border Murazzi than the patriotic and humane words of the old man had on the obstinate will of the two angry compatriots; and, with a certain aristocratic impulse of pride, the Prince exclaimed to his counsellor, "Retire!"

The seconds recommenced, with the same number of signals as before, and at the third, the adversaries marched towards one another, with pistol cocked in the right hand, with eyes unflinchingly fixed on each other, and with the deliberate intention of homicide.

About the twelfth step the Prince fired, his ball grazed the side of Morosini's neck; blood flowed, but the wound was slight.

The soldier of Calatafimi, cooler than his antagonist, approached closer. At about eight paces he fired, and the brother of Irene sank on the ground—the ball had pierced his heart.

The Holy Office of the Vatican laughed

at the news, with the infernal joy which
it experiences every time that blood shed
by private discord reddens the unhappy
soil.

And who spilt that Italian blood? An
Italian hand, alas! consecrated to the redemption of his country. How often it
has been thus!

CHAPTER LVIII.

On the second of December, the despot of the Seine, the false emperor, the enemy of all liberty, and the great ally of all tyrants, after seventeen years of unrighteous rule, pretended, with the same hypocrisy with which he kept her enslaved, to liberate the Niobe of nations, the old metropolis of the world—the ruler, the martyr, the glory of the earth.

He carried on the work of Divine vengeance. Attila, at the head of his ferocious tribes, had conquered Rome, destroyed her, and exterminated her people. Was not this God's justice?

"Whosoever sheddeth man's blood, by man shall his blood be shed!"

The ancient Romans ruled the world by subjugating the remotest nations, pillaging and breaking them down. Slavery, misery, and ruin, their ministers, compelled the nations of the earth to submit to their tyrants.

The successor of the Attilas, not less a robber than they, threw himself on an easy prey, and his false heart beat with joy when he clutched the victim. Yet even this action was but a caricature of the actions of the Attilas who have pillaged Rome. To accomplish great deeds, even of the evil sort, there must be great hearts, and *he* has a heart both little and cowardly. In all he does, we can see he intends to imitate his uncle; but the want of genius and energy makes the attempt a failure. Attila conquered, and made a pile of ruins of the proud victress-city. The modern Attila, in a Jesuit guise, did not destroy, did not ruin, because he considered the prey as his own property.

Afterwards, enfeebled by advancing years and luxury, his throne shaken to its foundation, he renewed his sinister undertakings in America, where he attempted to deal a death-blow to the sanctuary of the world's liberty—the great Republic—by building an Austrian empire at her gates.

And the Italian Government has accepted the bidding of the false emperor, acting as the sbirro of the Vatican, to hinder the Romans from liberating themselves, obliging them to submit to the control of the Holy Office, to deny to Italy her capital, though proclaimed by her parliament.

We firmly believe that a more cowardly Government than the Italian cannot be found in ancient or modern history. It must be accepted as the fate of humanity to find ever side by side with so much good so much evil, humiliation, and wickedness. We say side by side, because it cannot be denied that the unity of Italy is a marvel of good accomplished, in spite of all the efforts made by rulers and selfish factions to hold back this unfortunate country, by impoverishing and perverting it, and by every means of depredation and deception.

But what a Government! Can, indeed,

this agency of corruption be called a Government? And the unhappy people! what are they? Half of them bought over to hold the other half in bondage and in misery.

Hail, brave Mexicans! We envy your valour and constancy in freeing your land from the mercenaries of despotism! Accept, gallant descendants of Columbus, from your Italian brethren, congratulations on your redeemed liberty! On you was to be imposed a like tyranny, and you swept it away, as a noble and free river sweeps away impurity.

We alone—talkative, presumptuous, vain, boasting of glory, liberty, greatness—are yet enchained!—blindfolded, freeing ourselves with words, but unfit to accomplish by deeds that political reconstruction which alone would give us the right to sit down beside the other free nations.

Trembling before the despotism of an unscrupulous foreign tyrant, we dare not, for fear of him, walk about in our own homes, tell the world we are our own masters, or tear from our wrists the fetters which he has fixed there; and, more humiliating and degrading still, he has left the prey, which the indignation of the world forbade his appropriating, and has said, "Keep her, cowards; become cut-throats in my stead; but beware of meddling with my will!"

Oh, Rome! Thou who art truly "the only one!" Rome the eternal! Once above all human greatness! And now—now, how degraded!

Thy resurrection must yet be a catastrophe and a revolution to shake the rest of the world!

CHAPTER LIX.

THE stains of slavery are only to be finally washed out with blood.

The more intelligent and wealthy classes ought once for all to understand this, and to spare humanity the false solutions which settle nothing.

In other days, Venice, following the impetus given by her sister Lombardy, effaced the many years of her humiliation and servility in blood. It is not so now. She emerges from foreign dominion, not through her own acts, but by the courage of others. Oh! if only her liberty had been won by the valour of her brethren! But no, she was redeemed by foreign swords. Sadowa, the glory of Prussia freed Venice, and the Italian nation asks no veil to hide this dishonour.

Nations, like individuals, require dignity to live—require the life of the soul besides mere physical existence, to which our rulers would condemn us.

Once the Queen of the Adriatic carried her proud lion into the far east, repressed the victorious Ottoman, and dictated laws to him. The monarchs of Europe, invoked and backed by the jealous Italian States, conspired together against Venice, and were driven off by the amphibious and brave republicans.

Who would now recognise those proud compatriots of the Dandoli and the Morosini in the ranks of men who require the foreigner to free them; and, when free, throw themselves among the off-scourings of "the Moderates,"—a party ready for any abasement, for any infamy.

How tyranny alters the noblest beings, and emasculates them! Take comfort, however, Venetians; you do not stand alone, for such as you have I seen the descendants of Leonidas and Cincinnatus.

Slavery impresses on the forehead of man

such a mark of infamy as to confound him
with the beasts of the forest.

However, humbled as they have been,
and still are, the Italians do not neglect
their amusements and their festivals.
"Bread and pleasure!" they cry to their
tyrants, as of old they cried to their tri-
bunes; and the priest, to please, cheat, and
corrupt them, has surrounded himself by a
mass of ostentatious ceremonies, surpassing
all that the impostors of old furnished, to
conceal fraud by magnificent display.

Do not talk of politics, do not even think
of them, but pay, and despoil yourselves
with a good grace, so as to support your
masters richly, then they will give you to
satiety masses, processions, festas, games,
amusements, and sensual pleasures.

The sailing of the Bucentaur was one of
the ceremonies very dear to the people
when Venice was free—when it had its own
government and doge.

On the day fixed for the festival, the
Bucentaur, the most splendid galley of the
Republic, decked out with as much orna-

ment and as many banners as possible,
glittering with gilding and rich hangings,
bore the doge, the ministers of state, and
the most remarkable beauties of the day,
all in gala costume. They started from
the palace of St. Mark, and rowed towards
the Adriatic. Many other galleys formed
a procession, following in the wake of the
Bucentaur, as well as a large number of
gondolas decked for the holiday, and containing the largest part of the population,
male and female.

Oh, beautiful wert thou in those days,
ill-fated Queen! when thy Dandoli, thy
Falieri, sought, in the name of Venice, to
propitiate the waves on behalf of the bold
navigators of the Adriatic! Hail to thee,
Republic of nine centuries! true mother
of Republics! Yet if in thy greatness
thou hadst associated with thine Italian
sisters instead of hating them, the foreigner
could not have trodden us all down and
enslaved us as now.

Hide the wounds that your chains have
made, smooth the lines that misery has

impressed on your forehead. Do not forget, whether rejoicing or sorrowing, those humiliations through which you have passed, and henceforth remember that only when united can Italy defy the great foreign powers who are jealous of her uprise.

General Garibaldi stood leaning against a balcony of St. Mark's Palace, which looked over the lagoon, in the company of our fair Romans, with Muzio, Orazio, and Gasparo. He was listening to an old cicerone, who was dilating on the ancient glories of the Republic, and after having spoken on a variety of subjects, this individual had arrived at the description of the festival of the Bucentaur. He expressed his regret at not being able to see one of them now-a-days, and pointed to the spot whence from the mole started the famous craft, when suddenly Muzio's eye was arrested by a well-known face, which appeared at the entrance of the cabin of a gondola drawn up at the gates of the palace. Muzio disappeared like lightning, and stood before Attilio, who descended, pressed his friend's right hand, and could only articulate the melancholy word, "*Dead!*"

"It was fated then, that this relic of Roman greatness should come here to die," murmured the ex-President, having partly heard, partly guessed the tidings of Attilio.

"He died like a brave man," said the chief of the Three Hundred.

"And many Italians know how to die so," thought Muzio; "but it is sweeter to die fighting against the oppressors!"

"I will return to our party," said Muzio, "and consult with the General, that he may turn our excursion in another direction, so as not to expose Irene and Orazio to the shock of meeting the remains of their beloved one; I will afterwards rejoin you with Gasparo."

CHAPTER LX.

THE BURIAL.

Foscolo has these lines—

> A stone to mark my bones from the vast crop
> That death sows on the land or in the sea.

Admiring the mournful poems of this great singer, we are, like him, advocates for honouring the great dead; and truly, we believe, that doing homage to departed virtue is an incentive to make the living follow in its path. When one thinks, however, of the gaudy pageants with which the priesthood deck the last journey of the dead, one cannot help deploring the useless show and the expenditure.

Death, that true type of the equality of human beings—death which effectually destroys all worldly superiority, and confounds in one democracy of decay the

emperor and the beggar—death, the leveller,
must be astonished at so much difference
between the funerals of the rich and
the poor! He must wonder at so much
preparation for the burial of a corpse,
and laugh, if death can laugh, at so much
mockery of woe, which is frequently the
cover for secret joy in the soul of the
greedy heir, while in the largest number
it is mere indifference. Then the hired
weepers—what a pitiful spectacle those are!

We have seen in Moldavia, and we believe
the custom is adopted in other countries,
that at the funeral of a Bojar a number
of women are hired to weep, and what
tears they shed! what shouts do those
miserable beings utter! As to the grief
they must have felt, it was measured by
their pay.

These mourners have sometimes returned
to our memory while reading parliamentary
debates, during which certain hired people,
or those who hope for hire, burst out into
a profusion of " bravi " and " bravissimi "
at the insulting speeches, or often at the

unprincipled projects of this or that prime minister.

Prince T——'s funeral was largely attended, because it was known that he was a man of mark. Among the crowd of people who followed the remains, most of them with the greatest indifference, there could be distinguished a few really sad faces. Those were the friends of the dead man, Attilio, Muzio, and Gasparo. The latter especially had eyes swollen by weeping.

The strong nature of the old Roman chief had been shaken by the loss of his friend and master, to whom he had been sincerely attached—a proof at once of the kindly nature of the prince, and of the faithful heart of the exile. Was he weeping for the prince? No; for the friend and benefactor. Oh, how many true friends might the great of the world possess, if they would but open their hearts to generosity—if they would soften the injustice of fate towards those upon whom she lays an unequal hand!

Many there are among the higher classes, we know, who are beneficence itself, and some of the women of the noblest houses are distinguished for their amiability and goodness. But the good deeds of a few are not sufficient for the suffering multitude; and the majority of the favourites of fortune are not only indifferent to the unfortunate —they seem to add voluntarily to their trials.

The duty and the care of good government should be to ameliorate the poor man's condition; but, unhappily, that duty is unfulfilled, that care is not undertaken. Government thinks only of its own preservation, and of strengthening its own position; to this end it exercises corruption to obtain satellites and accomplices.

The mass of the prosperous might, to a great extent, mitigate the evil of maladministration by relieving misery and improving the condition of the people. If the rich would thus only deprive themselves of but a small portion of their superfluities! While the poor want the very necessaries of existence, the tables of the great groan with endless varieties of food, and the rarest and most costly wines. Does the rich man never feel the compunction of conscience which such shameless contrasts ought to bring?

"Why such grief for the loss of one of our enemies, capitano?"

These words were accompanied by a tap on Gasparo's shoulder, both proceeding from an odd-looking man, who was following in the funeral procession. Gasparo turned round, stood for a moment considering his familiar interlocutor, then uttering an exclamation little suited to the solemnity of the scene, and very surprising to those around him—"Evil be to the seventy-two! (a Roman oath) and is it really thee, Marzio?"

"Who else should it be, if not your lieutenant, *capitano mio?*"

The acquaintance of Gasparo had the type of the regular Italian brigand. The old man, during the few months of his city life, had somewhat re-polished his ap-

pearance; but Marzio, on the contrary,
presented the rude aspect of the Roman
bandit pure and simple. Tall and squarely-
built, it was difficult to meet without a
shudder the fierce look darted from those
densely black eyes. His hair, black and
glossy as a raven, contrasted with his
beard, once as dark, now sprinkled with
grey. His costume, though somewhat
cleaner, differed in other respects very
little from that rustic masquerade worn
when he had filled the whole country
with terror. The famous doublet of dark
velvet was not wanting, and if there were
not visible externally those indispensable
brigand accessories, pistols, dagger, or a
two-edged knife, it was a sign that those
articles were carefully hidden within.
Hats are worn in different fashions, even
by brigands, and Marzio wore his a little
inclined towards the right side, like a
workman's. Leathern gaiters had been
abandoned by Marzio, and he wore his
pantaloons, loose ones of blue, with ample
pockets.

The occasion did not offer the two men much opportunity of conversation; but it was evident that they met with mutual pleasure and sympathy.

In these times, when Italian honour and glory are a mockery, the handful of men called brigands, who have for seven years sustained themselves against one large army, two other armies of carabiniers, a part of another army of national guards, and an entire hostile population—that handful of men, call them what you will, is at least brave. If you rulers, instead of maintaining the disgraceful institution of the priests, had occupied yourselves in securing the instruction of the people, these very brigands, instead of becoming the instruments of priestly reaction, would at this moment have been in our ranks, teaching us how one stout fellow can fight twenty.

This, our kind word for the "honest" brigands, is not for the assassins, be it understood. And one little piece of comment upon you who sit in high places. When

you assaulted the Roman walls—for religious purposes of course — robbing and
slaying the poor people who thought you
came as friends, were you less brigands?
No, you were worse than banditti—you
were traitors.

But you will tell me, "those were republicans and revolutionists, men who
trouble the world." And what were you
but troublers of the world, and false
traitors? This difference exists between
your majesties and the bandit: he robs,
but seldom kills, while you have not
only robbed, but stained your hands for
plunder's sake in innocent blood!

Pardon, reader, that this digression has
left you in the midst of a funeral, and that
the writer has too passionately diverged
from his path to glance at brigandage on
the large as well as the small scale.

When the funeral party reached the
cemetery, the remains of the dead were
lowered into a grave, over which no voice
spoke a word of eulogy. With all the
will to effect good, the action of this

young life had been cut short by a premature and rash death.   What could be said of the blossom of noble qualities to which time was denied to bring forth their fruits?

CHAPTER LXI.

THE NARRATIVE OF MARZIO.

WE will leave our friends occupied in consoling the afflicted Irene for the loss of her brother, whom she had sincerely loved.

The last of a proud race! This thought would press upon the mind of the fair lady, who, despite her willingness to form a plebeian alliance, still valued, as we have seen, the high rank of her family.

Of the personal fortune which came to her through her brother's death she had not thought, for she was of too generous a nature to mingle an idea of interest with the life or death of a beloved object. The prince's family property, besides, which was in the Roman territory, had been confiscated by those worthy servants of God, whose possessions are " not of this world."

It was not until the friends had returned from the funeral that Attilio and Muzio had consulted with the General about imparting to the sister the knowledge of the fatal catastrophe. The . General, calling Orazio and his wife into his room, then first informed them gently of the sad occurrence.

Gasparo, who, with the exception of Irene, grieved the most, found some relief for his sorrow in the newly-acquired society of his former lieutenant. He was also full of the desire to hear the adventures of the man whom he had thought lost for ever. The two *ci-devant* banditti closely shut themselves up in Gasparo's room at the Victoria Hotel, at first conversing eagerly in interrogations and answers, nearly all monosyllabic, oratory not being the forte of brigands, who are more accustomed to deeds than words. After a time, the lieutenant began the following consecutive narrative :—

"After you had informed me, *capitano mio*, that you were tired of a forest life, and felt disposed to return to a private one, I

continued my usual mode of existence,
without ever deviating from the plan of
action you had enjoined, which was to
despoil the rich and the powerful, and to
relieve the needy and wretched. Our companions, formed in your school, gave me
little cause to reprove them; but if one
failed in duty, I punished him without
pity; and thus, by the grace of God, we
lived for several years. The charms of
womankind were always the rock on which
our hearts split; and well you know it,
capitano."

At these words, Gasparo began pointing
to his snow-white moustache, doubtless
remembering more than one gallant adventure in his career of peril.

The lieutenant continued: "You remember that Nanna, the girl that I adored, and
on whose account I was so much persecuted
by her parents? Don't for a moment
suppose that that dear creature betrayed
me; no, her soul was pure as an angel's."
And the bold bandit chief put his hand
to his eyes.

"She is dead, then!" exclaimed Gasparo.

"She is dead," repeated his companion; and a long silence followed.

Presently Marzio continued: "One day my Nanna, who was not well, had remained to pass the day in Marcello's house, where lived that poor Camilla, who had been violated and driven mad by the Cardinal P——. As I had to accompany my men on an important affair, the dwelling was attacked in the night, and my treasure carried off to Rome.

"I was maddened, but not a stone did I leave unturned till I had discovered the place in which they had hidden Nanna. At last I learnt, through friends in that city, that the poor child was in the convent of St. Francis there, and that they had condemned her to serve the nuns, and never to see the light again.

"My wife in the service of nuns, in the service of betrayed young women and of old foxes! 'I will give you a servant!' I said to myself; 'and by heaven the devil shall have the convent and the wretches it holds.'

"'The night following I entered Rome alone; it seemed to me a cowardly action to have companions in an undertaking which concerned none but myself.

"I bought a large bundle of dried branches in the Piazza Navona. I deposited them in a tavern, and waited till it grew late. Towards eleven o'clock, just before the house closed, I took my burden and hurried off towards 'St. Francis.' Who can prevent a poor wretch from carrying a bundle of wood home? Besides, Rome has one good point, which is that at night no one goes about for fear of the thieves, who are permitted, by the liberality of the priestly government, to do just as they please, as long as they do not interfere in politics.

"Having deposited my bundle at the gate of St. Francis, I pressed it closely in, prepared a box of lights to strike, and gave a searching look up and down the road.

"As will be easily understood, after the door was burnt, there would still remain the gratings, which would leave me pulling a very long face, and with little done. I was, therefore, obliged to make a noise, to attract the attention of those within. I then crossed the little square, and hid myself in a doorway, awaiting the appearance of some one, or at least a patrol. I had not long to wait, for after a few minutes I heard the measured tread of the patrol. Then, with that swiftness of foot which you know me to possess——"

Here Gasparo put in, "I should think I did! I remember that lord bishop who, having seen us at a distance on the road to Civita Vecchia, turned his horses, and set them in a gallop towards Rome, when you, in about the same time which I take to tell it, were already at the horses' heads, and had stopped the carriage."

"And what a take that was, captain," said the lieutenant. "How we did enjoy ourselves! how prodigal we were with our money for some time afterwards—I mean with the proceeds of the poverty of the descendant of the Apostles. But let us return to our story.

"I flew to the bundle of wood, set it on fire, and returned to my hiding-place. In a few minutes a great blaze lit the convent gate, and soon afterwards we had a sight equal to that which the crater of a volcano shows. And the police? The sorriest rabble everywhere, but in no place have they reached such scoundrelism as in Rome. The police, naturally cowards and slow of movement, instead of running to the spot to extinguish the flames, began shouting and making a tremendous noise to arouse the neighbourhood. Near the fire they never went, until a goodly number of people appeared at the doors, and then hurried to the scene of action.

"'It is now my turn,' said I to myself, and I rushed into the *mêlée*. The nuns should have been pleased with such a champion to deliver them, surrounded as they were by a company of roughs.

"Matters could not, however, have progressed better. At the clamour from without, the nuns were not slow to awake, and the gratings flew open. They flew to the rescue themselves, with tubs, pails, basins of water—in fact, with any utensil they could lay their hands on. After pretending to assist in extinguishing the external flames, but with my eyes fixed on the interior, seeing all parties well occupied, I sprang in to the assistance of the nuns in their sanctuary. No sooner within, than I cast a searching glance upon the crowd of females assembled, and to the oldest, who appeared the Superior, I addressed myself. Grasping her arm, I exclaimed, ' Come with me ! ' I found more resistance in the old lady than I expected. At first she struggled, and would only walk by compulsion, collecting all her strength to oppose me ; then she began to scream, and I was obliged to take her in my arms and to cover her face with a handkerchief.

"I was getting away from the crowd all the time, and arriving before the door of a cell which I found open, I entered with my burden. There was a light in the room, and the bed had been occupied. I laid the abbess upon it, and locked the door.

"She was astonished but not alarmed. I never saw a demon with such courage. 'Where is Nanna?' I began, in a way to startle her. No answer. 'Where is Nanna?' I repeated, in a louder tone still. No answer. 'I will make you find your tongue, witch!' I cried; and drawing this bit of steel from my belt, I made it glitter before her eyes. Still no answer."

"By the Virgin," said Gasparo, "these abbesses are all alike, real demoniacs. At the defence of Rome in 1849, when it was needful to pass through the convent of the Sacred Heart, to occupy the walls, they kept me waiting with my company at the gate for hours without opening it. When the abbess received the Government order for us to pass, she tore it in pieces. It was only when we began to knock down the doors with our axes that she allowed us to enter."

"Such was this one," recommenced Marzio. "I was not in a humour to play; I wanted Nanna, and a hundred lives such as the one before me would certainly not

have stopped me from carrying out my
object.   Seizing her with one hand, clench-
ing my dagger with the other, I was just
touching her throat—not with the point
of my dagger, for fear it should slip, but
with a hair-pin from her cap—I could
easily see that the lady had no intention
to reach martyrdom, as she was already
beginning with—

" ' For God's sake———'

" ' My Nanna,' I cried, ' or I will send
you to keep Satan company.'

" ' For God's sake let me go.'

" I released her head. She breathed hard,
and passed her hand over her forehead.

" ' You ask for a young girl of a good
family, who came from Rome, and who has
been a fortnight in the convent?

" ' I believe her to be the one I seek,'
I replied.

" ' Then I will lead you to her, on the
one condition that you will cause no scandal in this sacred house.'

" ' I desire nothing but to take my wife
with me,' I answered.

"When somewhat recovered, she rose from the bed, and said, 'Come with me.' I followed her for some time, and arrived at a dark corridor. We descended several staircases, and by the light of a taper which I had lit (I always carried a taper with me), I discovered an iron-barred door. 'Poor Nanna,' I thought; 'what crime has the child committed that she should be thrown in this infernal den?'

"Having reached the bolted door, the abbess drew forth a key, and placed it in the lock. She turned it, and motioned to me to pull the door towards me, it being too heavy for her to move. I did what I was desired, without for a moment losing sight of my guide, whose company was too interesting for me to lose. On opening the door, I made the old lady enter first, and then followed. No sooner was I within, than a young dishevelled woman sprang on my neck, and clung to me desperately.

"'Oh, Marzio!' she exclaimed; and a flood of tears from my Nanna bathed my face.

"I am too much of a brigand not to take my precautions in an emergency. Though beyond myself with joy at the recovery of my darling, I nevertheless did not cease to keep my eyes on the old wretch, who, without a strict watch, would undoubtedly have escaped us.

"When the first moment of emotion had passed, clasping my treasure by the hand, I closed the door, and asked if there was another in her cell.   She answered 'No.' The abbess, who had heard my question, said—

"'There is another door, and you had better leave by that, so as not to meet the sisters, who are doubtless searching for me now.'

"Here a fresh incident arose.   Another young girl came forward in haste, and interrupted the discourse of the abbess.   I had seen something moving in the darkest corner of the prison cell, but pre-occupation and the circumstances of the moment had prevented my thinking of it.   All at once I perceived a young girl somewhere about the age of my Nanna. She hastened towards me, saying, with a voice of emotion—

"'Surely you will not leave me alone in this prison. Oh, sir, I will follow Nanna through life and to death itself!'

"'Yes, Marzio,' added Nanna, 'for heaven's sake don't let us leave my unhappy friend in this wretched abode. She was destined by the abbess to seem my companion, and to act as a spy; but instead of that she has been an angel of comfort to me. She was charged to sound me, to gain information about you, to learn all she could of your companions—in fact, every particular, and then to report all to the abbess.'

"'So then things are carried on thus,' thought I, 'in these laboratories of falsehood and hypocrisy.'

"'She was charged to watch me, threaten me, torment me, in fact, in case I refused to divulge your hiding-places, your habitual rendezvous, your projects; but instead of that, she told me everything, consoled, protected, reassured me, and said that she would rather die than injure me, or cause me any trouble.'

" ' Besides, yesterday, she saved me from the insults and violence of an infamous prelate, who introduced himself into this cell (no doubt by the help of that old wretch), and who even offered me bribes if I would listen to his wicked proposals. She saved me by rushing in and uttering loud cries.'

" ' In vain did they promise her liberty if she would induce me to comply with their wishes, but nothing have they ever been able to obtain.   During the day they compel us to do the vilest work of the cloister, and at night they shut us up in this unclean den.'

" Tears again flowed down the lovely face of my dear one, while she uttered these words, and I assure you, captain, that my hand instinctively touched my dagger, with a wild wish to revenge Nanna's wrongs.

" I don't know how I restrained myself, for I was furious ; I could have annihilated the vile being before me, but it was well I did not, for without her I should never again have seen the light of heaven. 'Where is the second door you speak of, whither does it lead?' I demanded.

"'It leads outside the convent,' she replied, 'remove that iron bed which stands in the corner, and I will show you.'

"I removed it, but saw nothing.

"'Try to stir the bricks where the mortar looks damp.'

"Taking hold of an iron bar from the bedstead, I began to remove the bricks indicated. Finally I discovered a ring in a piece of wood, which showed the existence of a trap-door. I lifted the trap, and was surprised to find a staircase below. 'I must arrange the order of march,' said I to myself, 'and make the old witch the leader.' I then desired my young companions to follow, and giving one taper with little ceremony to the abbess, said to her, 'Forward!'

"'This then,' thought I, 'is the secret stair; and how many black deeds have been

committed in these labyrinths ? Ah, poor
deluded people, who fancy you are sending
your daughters to be educated in asylums
of purity when you place your children in
convents !

CHAPTER LXII.

MARZIO continued: "The old abbess walked in front, I followed, and the young girls brought up the rear. We descended about fifty steps, and entered a rather spacious passage, which soon led us into a large room. I suppose it to have been large, for with the help of the feeble taper, I could scarcely distinguish the walls. We had gone about ten paces, when I seemed to hear lamentations. I stopped, in order to listen better, but when I recollected myself, and was moving on, looking forward to my guide, behold I was in utter darkness.

"My God! I sprang forward with such a leap as a tiger might have taken, when from its hiding-place in the forest it rushes on its prey. Darkness was all I caught In vain I turned round and round, my arms

M 2

stretched as far as they could extend, in the hope of meeting that woman fiend. I darted against the wall, and kept following it, at the risk of taking the skin off my hands, but I found no door.

" At length, after feeling about for some time, and being almost reduced to despair, I leant heavily against the wall, and felt it give way with my weight.

"Hope re-awoke; I rubbed my hands over that part of the wall, and found to my surprise that it was wooden, which fact had escaped me in my previous investigation. I pushed hard against the planks, and then felt something move, as if a door on its hinges; at the same time a rush of offensive pestilential air entered by the aperture. I turned my head away to escape the putrid odour. The moans which I had before heard, again smote my ear, and calmed my agitation with wonder and pity.

" I thought of my companions, and remembered a few matches which I had in my pocket, but which I had forgotten in my excitement. I struck one of them, and looking at what I had supposed to be a door, found that it was a turn-table, and, Eureka ! at the bottom lay my taper, which the old wretch had dropped in her flight.

"When I had rekindled my taper, I found my companions near me, trembling like leaves. 'Courage !' said I, and threw myself into the adjoining apartment, they following, in the hope of overtaking the abbess, who had doubtless escaped this way. I hastened on, but, great God, what was my horror ! against the wall of the room through which I was flying, hung several human beings by the neck, the waist, and the arms, all but one dead, and more or less decomposed. The solitary survivor was a young man, once of a fine form, but now an emaciated phantom. He was wildly gazing at me, with deep, dark, open eyes, that seemed ready to burst from their sockets. He had ceased to moan, conscious that I had discovered and was approaching him. Whatever the danger of my own position, I could not leave that victim without making some attempt to

liberate him.   I approached, and kissed
him on the forehead; I always feel drawn
towards the suffering.   Surely the Almighty
inspires one with this sympathy, which is
not imparted by the poisonous breath of
the priest!—Well, well, let them call me
a brigand !

"Yes, I kissed the unhappy creature's
forehead, dropping sweat, yet burning like
a coal.   But what could I do for him? his
chains were soldered into the wall, and
those walls were massive.   I looked among
the dead, to see if I could find any iron
implement with which to excavate the wall,
or to break the chains.   Horrible! in every
direction were instruments of torture—bed-
steads, stretchers, pincers, ropes, gridirons,
&c., 'for the mortification of the flesh,' as
the priests say, but which fiends alone could
have invented, one would think, for the
torment of mankind.

"Nanna and Maria—such was the name
of Nanna's companion—had also drawn
near the unhappy youth, and endeavoured,
but in vain, to help him to escape from

his frightful position. Happily for us all, Nanna startled me with the exclamation, 'Oh, a key!' and truly, being very sharp-sighted, she had discovered a key in the loose mortar.

"Trying the key in the padlock of the chains, I found it fitted, and while the rusty locks yielded to my hand, my heart dilated. I was at the last chain, it fell, and I was freeing the youth's stiff limbs, when Nanna clasped me by the arm, and timidly pointed to a light in the direction of the wheel-door.

"I left my liberated companion, and in an instant stood at the entrance. No sooner was I there than I perceived one of the already-mentioned patrols, who was turning round the door, with his dark lantern in one hand, his pistol in the other. Shrinking into as small a space as possible, I stood back watching him. When his startled eyes were fixed on my face, which did not look pleasant at that moment, I had already grasped him by his right with my left hand, and my dagger was sheathed in his body.

He fell dead on the ground. You know, captain, that I am an enemy of blood-shedding, and that I never have spilt any except in self-defence; but in that instance there was no time for consideration. I knew there were others following the first, and I was one alone. The youth I had liberated showed signs of regaining power of exertion, and my brave female companions had succeeded in separating two bars from a torture bedstead, and stood behind me, ready to help. The situation was altered, yet the dead man, although I had despatched him noiselessly, had not expired without a cry. His companions, however, were frightened, and effected their escape. By keeping in absolute silence we could hear their steps in the distance. I repeat, there was no time to lose, or to hold councils of war before deciding on our course. To leave by the way we had entered was madness; still what other path remained? We all knew, however, that Roman catacombs have many outlets—this instance was not an exception.

" A look at my new companion confirmed me in my opinion that he was not useless to us, and without uttering a word, touching his heart with his hand, he made me understand that I could rely on him to follow me through all dangers.

" By this time daybreak must be at hand, and, doubtless, preparations were making in the convent to secure our capture. The likeliest conjecture was, that there were armed men placed at every outlet.

" The addition of the rescued man was very valuable to us all. He was not only acquainted with the subterranean path, but at a short distance he gathered up some torches, and distributed one to each of us. This was very useful, because my taper was almost extinguished, and the lantern which I had taken from the dead patrol, had not sufficient oil to last during the underground journey which was about to commence. To the right of the spot where the young man found the torches, he pointed out to me a light, and said, ' That opening leads to the garden of the convent,

and once passed, we are out of danger of
being intercepted.'

"On we went, I really think for two hours,
although we were in a subterranean road,
cut in the hard clay, of which you know,
captain, our Roman undersoil is largely
composed: and how many of those catacombs have we not visited together!

"Young and active, our two companions
were always near us. I frequently asked if
they were tired, or if they required support.
'Oh, no; go on! We will follow you, if it
be to death,' answered both girls.

"'There is the light,' finally exclaimed
Tito, for such was the name of the youth,
and, truly, before us appeared a bright point
in the distance. 'By that gate we shall
enter the woods of Guido Castle, whence
they dragged me, to conduct me to a seminary in Rome, the focus of all immorality
and vileness. Accursed be the hypocrites!'

"Arrived at the end of the subterranean
road, Tito began to clear away some
branches of lentisk which obstructed the
gate, and went out, looking first in all

directions. 'Safe!' he at last exclaimed,
'safe, so far—our persecutors have not
arrived!'

"When I got out with my companions, I
wondered how such a narrow and almost
imperceptible opening, when covered with
branches, could be the passage to such
spacious catacombs. 'Guido Castle!' said
I to Tito. 'Not far from here must be the
dwelling of the shepherd poet!'

"'Yes,' he replied, 'it is a few miles off,
and I will lead you straight to it; there we
can find a little rest, and food to satisfy our
hunger.'

"The sun of March was high above the
horizon when we left the underground
gloom, yet the change was not very
great, for in the beautiful forest in which
we found ourselves, the trees of centuries
gave no admission to the sunshine. The
paths formed by the passage of animals
were delightfully shady, and we should
have enjoyed our walk if we had suffered
less from fatigue and hunger. At last,
on the edge of the wood, appeared to the

longing eyes of our wearied travellers the cottage sought for, and fortunately we discovered our friend on the door-step. He seemed awaiting some one.

" ' Ah, Marzio !' exclaimed he, when we were near him, ' it was not you whom I expected to-day,' and we shook hands like old friends.

" 'I expected some of those government ruffians, because it was rumoured that men of your band were about the neighbour-hood. And,' he added, in a lower voice, drawing me aside, ' at a little distance from here is Emilio, with ten companies.'

" ' Instead of the hunters, you receive the game then, Lelio,' I said ; ' but a truce to talking, give us somewhat to eat and drink, for we are famished.'

" ' Come in, you will find all you want —ham, cream, cheese, bread, and real Orvieto. Eat and drink, while I keep a look-out for the Papal hounds. No questions now.'

" We ate the timely and abundant meal, and our first cravings satisfied, I asked Tito for the narrative of his adventures, which he gave in a few words.

"'I am,' he began, 'the son of Roman parents. My father, steward of the immense possessions of Cardinal M——, by the advice of his Eminence, sent me to a Roman seminary at the age of fifteen, to embrace the ecclesiastical career. For two years, contrary to my inclination, I was compelled to continue that detested life. For at first Father Petrucchio, the director of the seminary, showed me a good deal of sympathy, much to the vexation of my companions, who did not fail to be envious of my good fortune. The Father sometimes took me out with him to walk. These promenades with Petrucchio, in themselves somewhat tedious, appeared less so when I accompanied him to the convent of St. Francis, to visit the nuns. There the lady abbess and the nuns, pleased, I suppose, with my external appearance, used to compliment me and load me with attentions. The abbess, all-powerful over the director, obtained, without difficulty, that I should be em-

ployed in the religious service of the convent as assistant to the old priest who
officiated for the nuns. I was not long in
discovering that the abbess had conceived a
passion for me, and I became her too docile
favourite. For several months things
went on thus. Under one pretence or the
other, I was hardly ever seen in the seminary. I had the support of the director, so
I could do just what I liked, and he was
managed by the abbess, who, on that condition, left him certain licenses in her convent.
I, myself, inclined to anything but a seminary, was from boyhood passionately fond
of hunting, and any adventure that required
boldness ; and thus, during my excursions in
the neighbourhood of Guido Castle, I had
become acquainted with the subterranean
passage we have just left, and frequently I
have explored with torches its most hidden
recesses. Thus, indeed, I found a way of
communicating with the convent, and made
use of it to introduce myself there at all
hours, and by no means always at the invitation of the abbess. The history of her

jealousy would be too long. Cunning as I had been, she had not failed to discover my partiality for certain younger sisters, and many a time I have found her in such a towering rage as to make me tremble at her. The enormities that I witnessed in that den of iniquity cannot be recounted now. Many lives in the bud, or just unfolded, were there cut short! Things happened at which any pious soul would shudder. I, ashamed of myself, resolved to leave that pestilential place, never to return to it again. But I was doomed to pay the penalty of my complicity in so much abomination, for that old witch, the promoter of all licentiousness, appeared to have guessed my intention of flying, and did not give me time to accomplish my resolve. She one day said to me, " Tito, go down to the subterranean passage and bring me some torches; I have been asked for some for a midnight procession." I had a presentiment of misfortune; but there flashed across my mind the idea of taking advantage of the opportunity to leave for ever the den of impurity. No sooner had I reached the bottom of the staircase than I felt myself overpowered by four strong men, and dragged towards the charnel-house which you know, and from which I was so miraculously saved by you. They were sworn agents, and therefore my supplications, my grief, my promises were useless. I was as good as counted among the victims of vice and infamy when you saved me, brave man!' and Tito finished by kissing the hand of the bandit.

"Tito's story being ended, I felt a strong desire to hear something of Nanna's experiences; but, comforted and refreshed as we were by a draught of good Orvieto, and yet fatigued still by the extraordinary adventures we had passed through, we were all growing heavy-eyed, and by mutual consent we dropped asleep on our seats. I do not know how long we remained in that sleeping position, but a sharp whistle resounding through the dwelling made us start up. We were scarcely roused when the shepherd entered and said, 'Do not fear! My son Vezio has placed a sentinel on the top of the Petilia ruins, from whence whoever approaches can be distinguished. Those who are coming are our own people from your band.'"

And Marzio, as though he had not been in the presence of his captain, but in the Campagna, here stroked his jet black moustachios, thinking of those stout fellows.

"They were in fact our intrepid comrades," he went on, "the terror of the wretched priests. I leave you to imagine, captain, what our joy was on finding ourselves among those brave hearts. Many were the glad embraces given me by those whom the vulgar think hardened in all cruelties, but who are often in truth the manliest part of the people—those, namely, who will not bear bad rule and injustice : that part of the people who, could they receive something better than the education given by the priests—that is to say, a moral, humanising, and patriotic training—would furnish heroes to Italy, and to the world the same examples of courage and virtue which our fathers gave.

"Having thus so wonderfully saved my Nanna, and finding myself once more among my comrades, I had every reason to be satisfied with my luck ; yet I must repeat your favourite saying, captain, 'Happiness on earth only exists in the imagination !' Your words are true ; I soon felt that they were so. You remember that rascally priest at San Paolo, who seemed to have become friendly to us, and on whom we lavished so much sympathy and kindness ? Well, the wretch was in love with my Nanna, and never did he forgive me for having won her affection.

"Don Vantano, with the diabolic cunning which distinguishes his fraternity, had succeeded in ingratiating himself with the family of Nanna, and in poisoning their minds against me. Her four brothers—as I learnt from her—helped by others, devised the plot, and, under the guidance of the priest, succeeded in carrying off my darling from Marcello's house. Such was the brief story of Nanna. Being obliged again to absent myself with my men, and my dear

one being in a delicate condition, I resolved
to leave her in the charge of our host, with
Maria as a companion. They had become
as sisters, their affection being strengthened
and cemented by the dangers and trials
they had shared. Still, being ever uneasy
as to the fate of my beloved, and well aware
of the malice of her persecutor, I kept
wandering about Lelio's neighbourhood, as
the lioness who deposits her young, while
she goes in search of food, always encircles
the hiding-place of her treasure. I felt
certain that it would be very difficult for
those who had at first carried off Nanna to
effect that object a second time. I was
well assisted in guarding her by Tito,
who knew those parts thoroughly, and
who attached himself to me with much
gratitude.

"Still, what height cannot the wickedness of a priest reach! Vantano, knowing
how hazardous it would be for him to
carry off his prey, determined to destroy it!
Being near her confinement, the unhappy
child, alone with the inexperienced Maria,

followed the advice innocently given her by Lelio, to call in a midwife from Guido Castle—a woman who till then had borne a good character for honesty. But who can reckon on the honesty of a woman where bribery and monkery reign! He who does not believe my words, let him but pass a few months in the nest of those hypocrites, sitting in the places that once held a Scipio and a Cincinnatus.

"How many crimes may not a weak woman be induced to commit when she is assured that she is fulfilling God's will, and listening to God's word. God's word!— sacrilege of which a priest alone would be guilty. At every ceremonial the Catholic faithful go to receive God's oracles from the lips of the bride of Christ, the Church. She is no pure bride, but a secret harlot. By one of her ministers poison was administered to my Nanna, and thus was I robbed of wife, child, and every earthly happiness.

"I was arrested, torn from her cold body, myself almost unconscious of life. I learnt afterwards that my seizure required to

accomplish it a number of the Papal
mercenaries, and that our brave fellows
fought desperately in my defence till, overpowered by reinforcements, and nearly all
wounded, they retired in bold order.

"I was stupefied, and called again and
again on death, but in vain; the triumph
of my captors was made complete, for I
was alive and enchained. From the galleys
of Civita Vecchia I was, after several
months, sent to Rome, and subsequently
liberated, after being compelled to take an
oath to obey and maintain the authority
of the Pope—an oath to serve faithfully
an impostor and a despot, to swear to obey
him, even if the command were to murder
one's father and mother. And I swore—
I tell you the whole truth—but I swore
also along with it war on themselves, and
while this life lasts I am their enemy to
the bitter end."

PART THE THIRD.

CHAPTER LXIII.

THE CAIROLIS AND THEIR SEVENTY COMPANIONS.

A PEOPLE well-governed and contented do not rebel. Insurrections and revolutions are the weapons of the oppressed and the slave. The inciting causes of such are tyrannies. The apparent exceptions, originating from different circumstances, are, when closely examined, found to be the offspring of moral or material despotisms.

England, Switzerland, and the United States have experienced, and may still experience, insurrections, although these countries are by no means badly governed.

Switzerland has had her Sonderbunds, and England her Fenians. These latter are chiefly kept in vigour by the Romish priests, through the moral tyranny exercised by them over the most ignorant of the population in Ireland.

The United States have witnessed, in these latter years, a terrible revolution, caused by the material tyranny the rich colonists of the South exercised over their slaves, which they, moreover, desired to extend to the other States of the Union.

Moral or material tyranny is always the cause of revolution. And in Rome who can deny that both moral and material tyranny is exercised?

Yes, in Rome exists the twofold revolting despotism of the priests who lay Italy at the feet of the stranger; who sell her for their profit! Theirs is the most depraved of all forms of tyranny.

Picture a dreary, dark, windy, damp night in October. The rain has ceased to fall on the seething and foaming surface of the Tiber. The banks of the river are muddy and furrowed, for every ditch has become a torrent, and scarcely a vestige of dry and solid ground is perceptible.

In several boats behold seventy men, armed with poniards and revolvers, and a few miscellaneous muskets. Their habiliments were far too thin for that cold rainy night. But the Seventy were warmed by the heat of heroism.

Rome on this night was to rise in rebellion.

Many of the bravest youths from every Italian province had contrived to enter the city, and our old friends Attilio, Muzio, and Orazio, with their companions, were at their posts, ready to head the Roman rising.

In vain did the priesthood endeavour to discover the conspirators, arresting right and left all upon whom the slightest suspicion fell: their efforts were vain, for Rome swarmed with brave men, ready to sacrifice themselves in order to secure her liberation.

The Seventy, impelled by the current of the Tiber, were rapidly advancing to the assistance of their brothers. Under cover of Mount St. Giuliano, those valorous youths landed, at the hour of midnight, on the 22nd of October, 1867.

Enrico Cairoli led his heroic companions. "We will rest," he said, "our limbs in this Casino della Gloria, until we receive intelligence from our allies in the city, so that our attack may be made on the enemy simultaneously. Meanwhile," went on their leader, "I feel it my duty to remind you that this enterprise is a dangerous one, and therefore the more worthy of you. If, however, any of you are overdone, or feel at all indisposed to the great task, and do not care to follow us, let them return. We shall not think it a crime in them to do so; and all we say to them is, 'Farewell, till we meet in Rome!'"

"In life and in death we will follow you," answered, as in one voice, those intrepid youths, not one of whom turned back.

"The guide who was to conduct us to Rome is not to be found, and no one has yet returned to give us any news," said Giovanni Cairoli—who had just come back from an exploration—to his brother.

Dawn began to appear, and they were now in the wolf's mouth—that is, near the advanced posts of the Papal troops, and in danger of being attacked at any moment.

"What does it signify?" said Enrico Cairoli, in reply to his brother's remark. "We came here to fight, and we will not return without having accomplished that duty."

At mid-day a messenger arrived from Rome, and announced, "The movement on the previous evening had remained an imperfect one, and the conspirators were waiting for orders to direct them how to act."

The messenger was sent back to urge immediate internal agitation, and to assure them of the readiness of the Seventy to co-operate.

No answer was returned. At five o'clock in the afternoon, the Seventy being discovered, were attacked by two companies of the Papal troops. The valorous Giovanni Cairoli, who, at the head of twenty-four men, formed the vanguard, posted in a rustic house in the village, was attacked

first; and, notwithstanding the inferiority
of his numbers, withstood the assault of
the enemy.   His equally valiant brother
Enrico, the commander, seeing him in
danger, overcome by force of numbers,
charged to the rescue, and drove back the
mercenaries, who fled at the sight of these
brave and devoted boys.

Being reinforced by other companies, the
mercenaries entrenched themselves behind
the heights of Mont St. Giuliano, from
whence they kept up a fearfully destructive
fire with their superior arms.   The Cairolis,
with their intrepid companions, crippled by
the inferiority of their fire-arms, many of
which would not go off, resolved to charge
them at the point of the bayonet, and
made one of those assaults that so often
decide battles.   The mercenaries, completely
daunted, left upon the field their wounded
and dead.   The young soldiers of Liberty
lost their heroic chief and friend, and many
of them were seriously wounded.   Night
came, and put an end to that unequal but
gallant strife.

CHAPTER LXIV.

CUCCHI AND HIS COMRADES.

AND in Rome, what were Cucchi and his companions doing, and the Roman and provincial patriots consecrated to freedom and death? Cucchi, of Bergamo, was one of the most excellent men the revolution gave to Italy. Handsome, young, and wealthy, he belonged to one of the first families in Lombardy. Guezzoni, Bossi, Adamoli, and many others, despising the tortures of the Inquisition, and all other dangers, directed the Roman insurrection, under the command of that intrepid Bergamasco.

The unhappy Roman people received with obedience the directions of those valiant youths, and asked to be supplied with arms. Arms in plenty had been sent down to the Volunteers from all parts of Italy; but the Government of Florence, expert in every form of cunning, took means to stop them, so that there were very few weapons to be dispensed to the Romans.

Add to this the treachery prepared for this unhappy people, viz., the tacit promise that a few shots should be fired in the air, and that then the Italian army from the frontier would fly to their assistance. By such false pretences and underhand proceedings at Florence, the people of Rome, as well as their heroic friends, were deceived. Those shots were fired, but no help came for Italy.

Poor Romans! they fought with rude weapons in the streets against an immense number of well-armed soldiery, who were backed by armed priests, monks, and police. They succeeded in mining and blowing up a Zouave barrack, and with the knife alone fought desperately against the new-fashioned carbines of the mercenaries.

In Trastevere, our old acquaintances, Attilio, Muzio, Orazio, Silvio, and Gasparo, had re-united with all those remaining of the Three Hundred on whom the police had not laid their hands.* The people having thus found capable leaders did their duty. Some of the old carbines that had done execution in the Roman campaign now reappeared in the city in the hands of Orazio and his companions, who made them serve as an efficacious auxiliary to the Trasteverini's naked knife.

The city rose in its chains as best it could, and used an armoury of despair. Carbineers, Zouaves, dragoons on their patrol, were struck by tiles, kitchen-utensils, and many other objects thrown from the windows by the inhabitants, stabbed by the poniards of the Liberals, and wounded by shots from blunderbuss and firelock. Thus assailed, the troops fled from the Lungara towards St. Angelo's bridge, and passed it, though they were checked by the Papalini. The bridge was guarded by a battery of artillery, supported by an entire regiment of Zouaves. When the people, intermingled with those

* Ten thousand patriots, it is said, were arrested in Rome in this last movement, by the paternal Government.

whom they were pursuing, crowded on the
bridge, the commander of the *clericali* ordered his men to fire, and the six guns of
the battery, with the fire of the entire line of
infantry, poured out over the bridge, making
wholesale slaughter of the people and the
mercenaries.   What did his Holiness care
about the scattered blood of his cut-throats
and bought agents?   The money of Italy's
betrayers was at his service to purchase more.
What was of the greatest importance was
the destruction of many of his Roman children.   Many indeed were the rebels who
paid with their lives for their noble gallantry in venturing on that fatal bridge.
Many, truly, for in their enthusiasm the
people attempted three consecutive times to
carry it, and three consecutive times they
were repelled by the heavy storm of bullets
rained upon them, and the shots from the
cannon of the defenders of the priests.

It may well be supposed that, among
those who were at the head of the people
during this assault of the bridge, our five
heroes would be found fighting like lions.

After having consumed their ammunition, they had broken their arms upon the skulls of the Papal soldiery, and provided themselves with fresh ones by taking those of the killed. It was they who continued the assault at the head of the people, whom they excited to positive heroism.

It was, however, too hard a task. The first of the courageous leaders to bite the dust was the senior one, the venerable prince of the forest, Gasparo. He fell with the same stoicism which he had displayed during all his existence—with a smile upon his lips, happy to give his life for his country's holy cause, and for the cause of humanity.

A bursting shell had struck him above the heart, and his glorious death was instantaneous and without pain.

Silvio also fell by the side of Gasparo, both his thighs pierced with musket-balls. Orazio had his left ear carried off by a bullet, while another slightly grazed his right leg. Muzio would have been despatched also by a shot in the breast, had it not been for a strong English watch (a present from

the beautiful Julia), which was smashed to
atoms, and so saved his life, leaving the
mark of a severe contusion. Attilio had
his hip grazed, as well as his left cheek,
and received from a flying bullet a notch
on his skull, resembling in appearance the
mark a rope wears on the edge of a well.

The butchery of the people was so great,
and the fallen were so numerous, that after
these three consecutive charges the brave
insurrectionists were obliged to retreat.

Orazio carried Silvio on his back into the
first house near the bridge for safety, but
when the soldiery returned, the wounded
were massacred and cut in pieces.

Women, children, and many unarmed
and defenceless persons who fell into the
hands of these worthy soldiers of the priesthood shared a similar fate.

The good instincts of the working-class
are proved in the solemn times of revolution. In such times the noble-minded work-
ing-man defends his employer's property,
never robs him; but if he takes arms he
spares the lives of defenceless beings, and

of those who surrender. He would shudder to kill with the cynicism of the mercenary ; he fights like a lion—he who was so patient —one against ten !

In the Lungara there is a large woollen manufactory, which employs many workmen. From that woollen factory many had joined the insurgents, the elder ones remaining to guard the establishment.

When these good old artisans saw the people and their fellow-workmen thus followed by the Papal bullies and the mercenaries, they threw open the doors and gave shelter to the fugitives, or at any rate to some of them, and levelled bars, axes, and every iron instrument that would serve as a weapon of offence or defence against the hated foreigners and the gendarmerie.

There arose in consequence an indescribable tumult at the entrance to the factory, where the advantage was, at first, to the honest people, and where not a few of the Papal soldiers had their skulls smashed in, and their blood let out by the blows received. At length the besiegers took up

their position in the opposite houses, and
the besieged, having barricaded themselves,
and collected a few more fire-arms, began
afresh, with constant change of fortune, a
real battle.

Our three surviving friends had entered
the factory, and fought there with great de-
termination. The workmen and insurgents,
too, encouraged by their chiefs, had also
comported themselves valorously. But ammunition was lacking, and detachments of
mercenaries were advancing to the succour
of their comrades.

Night, however, now favoured the sons
of liberty, who, although without ammunition, still kept up the defence.

It was 7 P.M. when the fire of the insurgents ceased, and a division of Papal troops
commenced the assault. They began by
attacking the large front door of the factory,
which the workmen had barricaded but not
closed. Orazio and Muzio, after further
strengthening the entrance, armed each man
with an axe, and, picking out the youngest
and boldest Romans, stationed some of them

to the right and some to the left of the door
to defend it. Thus prepared for a desperate
resistance, determining to sell their lives
dearly, the assault was received.

Attilio had undertaken to defend the
other entrance, and keep off the second
portion of the assailants. Having secured
the back doors in the best manner possible
with his appliances, he placed a number
of workmen at the windows of the upper
floor, from whence they were to cast upon
the assailants whatever missiles could be
found. As soon as he had completed these
arrangements, he placed himself with his
friends at the most dangerous post, armed
with the sabre of a gendarme whom he had
slain during the day.

The internal appearance of the factory
presented at this moment a sad picture.
Many bodies of courageous citizens killed
in its defence had been carried to and
deposited in an obscure corner of its extensive courtyard. In other corners, lying
here and there, were the wounded, and some
were also stretched in the rooms upon the

ground floor. But not a groan was heard from these valorous sons of the people.

An immense table, with a candelabrum in the centre, occupied the middle of an extensive saloon on the left side of the front entrance to the building, and on that table could be seen heaps of bandages, slings, cotton-wool, and linen of various kinds—the best which the house could furnish for the use of the wounded. A large vessel of water was under the table —perhaps the most useful relief of all to the wounded sufferers, be it to moisten and cool their wounds by bathing, or to quench the feverish thirst which wounds generally occasion.

Three women of rare and noble beauty moved about in this improvised hospital, superintending the wounded, and we recognise in their gentle yet bold mien our three heroines, Clelia, Julia, and Irene.

The poor abandoned Camilla, ignorant of the loss of her Silvio, and with the traces of her past sorrows still lingering on her sweet face, mechanically assisted the three merciful women in their kind attentions to the sufferers.

They had awaited their friends in the factory with these preparations as soon as the battle on the bridge commenced, and they received the wounded when the people, driven back, sought refuge in the establishment, and entrenched themselves there. Other women of the people were on the spot also, tending the suffering, and carrying them what relief the circumstances permitted.

"Well, prince of the campagna," Attilio might be heard saying to Orazio, "we have seen many strifes, but the one we are in to-night is likely to prove the hardest of all. What consoles me is that our Romans seem to remember the olden times. Look at them, not one turns pale—all are ready to confront death in whatever form it may come."

"On the contrary," answered Orazio, "they laugh, joke, and are as merry as if they were taking a walk to the Foro to empty a foglietta.

" We have still some wine. Let us give
a draught of Orvieto all round to these our
brave comrades," exclaimed Attilio.

When all had refreshed themselves with
a glass of that strengthening cordial, a
unanimous and solemn cry of " Viva
l'Italia!" rolled forth like thunder from
that dense and resolute crowd of Rome's
desperate defenders.

CHAPTER LXV.

THE MONTIGIANIS.

WHILE the conflict in Trastevere was going on, the Montigianis, headed by Cucchi, Guerzoni, Bossi, Adamoli, and other brave men, did not remain with their hands folded. The explosion of the mine under the Zouaves' barracks was arranged as the signal for their movement. The mine exploded, and those noble fellows moved with heroic resolution at the head of all the youths that could be assembled.

As many of the agents and mercenaries frightened by the explosion as were met running away were disarmed by the people, and killed if they offered resistance.

The mine, however, had done little damage, though it made a great uproar. Either the quantity of powder was insufficient, or it was badly placed.

The clerical journals, or those of the Italian Government, which are much the same, have stated that only the band of the Zouaves, composed of Italian musicians, had been blown up, and that the foreigners, specially recommended to the efficacious prayers of his Holiness, had been miraculously saved.

The Italians, it is true, have not the good fortune to be the objects of modern necromancy's prayers; but the facts are these: A very few mercenaries were killed, and the others, having left the barracks and arranged themselves in order, had opened a sharp fire against the people. Cucchi, with his lieutenants Bossi and Adamoli, had marched to the barracks, and at their command, and animated by their example, the Roman youths had precipitated themselves furiously upon the foreign mercenaries. It was a hand-to-hand struggle of persons who for the greater part were unarmed, and who struggled against trained soldiers, from whom they endeavoured to tear away their weapons. But the mercenaries were

many. Gold and the help of Buonaparte
had been potent. A great number of
French soldiers, under the name of Papal
Zouaves, had crowded into Civita Vecchia
for a long time previous, in readiness to
start for Rome.

The resources that the Jesuits and *re-
azionari* had sent to the Pope from all parts
of the world had also been immense.
Added to this, a great number of fanatics,
priests, and monks,* disguised in the
uniform of the mercenaries, mingled with
the Papal troops, exciting them to heroism
and to slaughter, promising them as a reward the glory of heaven, as well as plenty
of gold on earth, and all they could desire.
Alas, poor Roman people! But whom
should we reckon under this denomination?
When one has excepted all the priestly portion, Pope, cardinals, bishops, priests, and
friars congregated there from all parts of
the globe, with their women, their servants,
their cooks, their coachmen, &c., with the

---

* Some were discovered among Garibaldi's Zouave
prisoners in Monte Rotondo.

relations of their domestics, the servants of their women, and, finally, a mass of the working-classes dependent on this enormously rich rabble, what is left? Those who remain, and are worthy of the name of "people," as not belonging to the necromancers, are some honest middle-class families, a few boatmen, and a few lazzaroni.

In the country, where ignorance is fostered by the priesthood, and has struck still deeper root, the people side with the clergy throughout Italy, but particularly in the Roman campagna, where all the landowners are either priests, or powerful friends of the priesthood.

To return, however. While Cucchi, at the head of his men, and aided by his brave companions, sustained a heroic but unequal combat outside the Zouaves' barracks, Guerzoni and Castellazzi, leading a company of youths, had assaulted the gate of San Paolo, disarmed a few guards, and succeeded in passing the court, inside of which was to be found a depôt of arms. The

arms were there, truly, but guarded by a
strong body of Papal troops and police,
with whom our valorous friends had to
sustain another extremely unequal combat;
and, being finally dispersed, were hotly
pursued by the furious Papalini.

CHAPTER LXVI.

THE OVERTHROW.

THE heroic Cairolis and their companions had meanwhile paid with their blood for their sublime patriotism and generous constancy to the Roman insurgents.

The morn of the 24th of October was tearful, dark, and dreary, the forerunner of fresh Italian misfortunes, and looked down upon the young and noble countenance of Enrico, "the new Leonidas," upon his brother Giovanni, lying in their blood, with many others belonging to that dauntless brigade. The first died with a smile of scorn upon his lips for that paid horde who had massacred them, ten against one. Giovanni, all but mortally wounded, was lying near the corpse of his beloved brother, surrounded by other sufferers whose glorious names history will register.

Few were the survivors of the valorous Seventy, and those few left the field of slaughter to unite themselves to their other brethren, who were combating at the same time against the foreign hordes outside the walls of Rome. Guerzoni's undertaking to seize the arms deposited outside the gate of San Paolo was conducted with the same intrepidity he had displayed in a hundred combats, but failed, for the plain reason that the Roman youths under his orders, being poorly armed, were compelled to give way before the blows of the mercenaries, and fly.

He and Castellazzi, after a thousand brave endeavours, were dragged off in the scattering of the people, and were forced to conceal themselves whilst they awaited a fresh opportunity to strike for Rome.

Cucchi, Bossi, and Adamoli, at the head of their detachments, performed deeds of great valour. They gained possession of a portion of the Zouaves' barracks, with only their revolvers and knives as weapons. Fights between the Papalists and the mob were frequent, and the latter, for want of other arms, beat the former to pieces with their sticks.

But here, too, they had to give way before superiority of numbers, discipline, and arms. Here also the first rays of daylight on the 24th presented to the view of the horror-struck passer-by a heap of corpses, mingled with dying men. In this manner was the tottering throne of the " Vicegerent of Heaven " consolidated— re-established by the butchery of the un- happy Roman people, and this, too, per- formed for hire by the scum of all nations, supported by the bayonets of Buonaparte's soldiers !

CHAPTER LXVII.

THE FINAL CATASTROPHE.

BUT the details of the fight at the factory must be given. The assault was imminent. "Ready, boys," exclaimed in one voice Orazio, Attilio, and Muzio; "Ready!" and the summons was scarcely pronounced when the Papalists threw themselves upon the front door of the manufactory. In the interior all the lights had been extinguished. On this account the Government troops, though seen by our side, could not distinguish individually any of the sons of liberty, and the first who attempted to scale the barricade fell back, their skulls split open by the terrible axes of Orazio and Muzio, or the sabre of Attilio, as well as by the different instruments of defence used by their valorous companions.

Yet, although they repulsed the enemy, the besieged sustained an important loss

in that first assault. A shot from a
revolver pierced the heart of the gallant
and intrepid Orazio, who, despising cover,
had exposed his person at the top of the
barricade to the enemy, and fell as he
clove one of them with his axe.

The "Prince of the campagna of Rome"
fell like an oak of his own forest, and his
strong right hand grasped his weapon
tightly even in death.

"Irene" was his last thought, and the
last word that escaped from his lips. Ah!
but Irene's soul was pierced by that dying
voice! for the three women, although they
took no part in the defence, remained at a
short distance only from those whose hearts
beat in unison with their own.

Irene first reached him whose beloved
voice had called her, and her two companions soon followed. As Orazio's body
remained upon the barricade where he
fell, the noble woman, heedless of her
danger, had directly scaled it, and her
beautiful forehead was struck at that
moment by a ball from a musket; for the

mercenaries, enraged at their bad success, were firing at random through the open door.

It may be imagined with what feelings the two surviving friends and their beloved ones had those precious bodies carried into the interior.

The factory had indeed become a charnel-house, it being useless for the chiefs to admonish their men to keep under cover.

There are moments when death loses its horror, and when those who would have fled before a single soldier take no heed of a shower of shots falling in every direction. Such was the case now with those poor and courageous working-men. Not counting the large number of troops by whom they were surrounded, nor the multitude firing in the direction of the door, they stood to their defences without precaution, and allowed themselves to be needlessly wounded. In this way the numbers of the defenders became lessened, whilst that of the dying and killed was momentarily augmented.

Attilio and Muzio saw at a glance how matters stood, and that there was nothing for it but to confront the enemy till death. Yet Clelia and Julia! why should they also die, so young, so beautiful?

"Go thou, Muzio," said Attilio, "and persuade them, while there is yet time, to escape by the back entrance, and place themselves in safety. Tell them that we will follow a little later."

In this last part of his speech the generous Roman prevaricated. He had already tasted all the glories of martyrdom, and would not have relinquished it even for Clelia's love.

But at this juncture who is it that has arrived as by a miracle, climbing like a squirrel in at a window, and appearing in the midst of that great desolation in these last sad moments? It is no other than Jack, our brave sailor Jack, saved from shipwreck by Orazio, to whom he had ever since been much attached! He found himself in Rome during the terrible occurrences which we have related, and at

the first occupation of the factory was sent
to ascertain the result of the insurrection in
various parts of Rome.

Jack returned with sad news. He, with
his English resolution, and with the agility
that characterised him, had assisted at
nearly all the fights, and shared in the
bad results.

Attilio and Muzio were now fully aware
of the fate that was reserved for them, and
they also learned that it was impossible for
the women to escape by the back premises
of the factory. To accomplish this they
would have needed the nimbleness and
agility of the young sailor.

Muzio, therefore, replied thus to his
friend's injunctions :—" I will tell the
ladies what you say ; but I believe first,
that it is impossible for them to leave; and,
secondly, that they would not leave us if
they could."

CHAPTER LXVIII.

THE SUBTERRANEAN PASSAGE.

AMONGST the surviving workmen who were
defending the large front entrance to the
manufactory was an old grey-headed man,
who listened intently to the above conversation of the two chiefs. When Muzio
uttered the last words, he exclaimed,
" *Coraggio, signors !* If you wish to retire
from this place, and to save the women, I
know of a passage that will lead us out
of danger."

A ray of hope broke upon the minds
of the two friends when they heard there
was a way of saving their beloved ones,
and they immediately proceeded to avail
themselves of it, for there was no time to
be lost, as the enemy was preparing for a
fresh attack.

Muzio approached Julia and Clelia, who

were not far off, and obtained a promise, on
the condition that he and Attilio would
soon follow them, that they would take
refuge under the escort of old Dentato and
Jack in the subterranean passage. The
other women would follow after them, and
lastly our friends with all the remaining
defenders of the factory.

And the wounded? Ah! if there be a
circumstance that is harrowing and terrible
in those butcheries of men called "battles,"
it is certainly that of abandoning one's own
wounded to the enemy!

Poveri! In one moment the faces of
your friends—of your brothers, who be-
wailed your hurt, who tended you with
such gentleness, will disappear, to be succeeded by the revolting, horrible, and
triumphant faces of the mercenaries. At
the best they will be brutal; at the worst,
they, infringing every right of war and of
people, will steep their base bayonets in
your precious blood! Cowards! who fled
before you, and to whom you so often
generously conceded their lives!

Supported by the 20,000 soldiers of the 2nd of December, they have regained once more their spirits, and have forgotten that they owe their ignoble existences to you.

In St. Antonio (America) Italians fought against the soldiers of despotism, and many, very many were wounded. There, carried on their brother's backs, or transported on horses, the wounded were removed. Not one was left alive* to be at the mercy of Rosa's cannibals.

And are the hirelings of the priests less cruel? At the station at Monte Rotondo, after the glorious assault of the 25th of October, three wounded men were lying awaiting the convoy that was to convey them to Terni, when the Pope's soldiers arrived. Worthy followers of the In-quisitors, they amused themselves with murdering our unhappy companions by stabbing them with their bayonets, and

---

* It is painful to state it, but one man, hopelessly wounded, was killed so that he should not be in the enemy's power, who usually cut the throats of those they found alive on the field.

giving them blows with the butt-end of their guns.*

Oh, Italians, leave not in your enemy's power your wounded! It is too heart-rending a spectacle. If they be not murdered, they will remain at least to be mocked and jested at by those who are accustomed to outrage Italy.

Attilio and Muzio, though tired and wounded themselves, would not abandon their helpless comrades to the insults and the steel of the priests' soldiers.

In the lowest part of the factory, at the extremity of an immense room used for washing the wool, was a massive oak door, which appeared at first sight to lead to a channel of water which discharged itself into the Tiber. The canal really existed, but the door we have referred to did not lead to it, but to a subterranean passage, gained by a bridge built across this same canal. Into this underground vault a procession of the devoted women, the wounded, and the workmen, began to defile.

* An historical fact.

But in the priestly city, where education consists in being taught to play the hypocrite and to lie, traitors abound. And a traitor threw from one of the upper windows of the factory a written paper, whilst these brave people were retiring, informing the soldiery of the retreat of the defenders.

The attack was no longer deferred, and an ever-increasing crowd of mercenaries and police threw themselves upon the barricade at the door, and rushed in.

Only a few defenders remained. Had Attilio and Muzio been more careful of themselves, and taken to flight, they might perhaps have saved their lives. But too lavish of their blood were this pair of noble Romans. They did not fly; they remained to fight desperately for some time against that in-pouring stream of slaves.

Many were the assailants cut down upon the heap of dying and of dead. But heroes, like cowards, have only one life. The assailants were too numerous, and side by side the valorous champions of Roman liberty fell together, and exhaled their last breath.

Dentato, who had assisted in this last struggle, seeing that all hope of a successful resistance was over, favoured by the darkness, and his acquaintance with the establishment, gained the washing-house, and thence the subterranean passage, closing the oak door from the outside upon that scene of blood, and barring it as well as he was able.

The hired assassins of the priesthood having no other motives than rapine and slaughter, inundated the factory with the hope of securing plunder and wreaking revenge. They never thought of the ' oaken back-door by which the surviving defenders of Italian liberty had escaped, until too late.

Having discovered by-and-by that the building contained only corpses, they were reminded of the subterranean passage. They searched, inquired, and at length discovered the door leading to it. Some time elapsed before they succeeded in forcing open the obstacles which barred it, as well as in organising an entry into the darkness, and all this gave the fugitives sufficient opportunity of escaping in safety.

In the first week of November, 1867, three females, an old man, and a lad in the bloom of youth, descended at the Leghorn station.

At the head of this party stood one of those daughters of England, from whose pure and lofty countenance, sad though she was, and dressed in mourning, the heart derived new ideas of the dignity and happiness of life.

Her lady companion was not less beautiful nor less sad, and displayed in the lovely lineaments of her face a different but exquisite feminine delicacy of the Southern type, such as Raffaele portrayed in his Fornarina.

The third woman was also comely; but sorrow had furrowed her forehead deeply, and a look of vacancy had settled upon her melancholy features. The old man, Dentato, whom Julia would not leave to misery and want, was occupying himself about the luggage.

Jack, with the vivacity of sixteen years, offered his arm to the ladies, to assist them as they alighted from the railway carriage. He quickly discovered Captain Thompson and his wife, the Signora Aurelia, who were awaiting them, and saluted the latter, who had a high regard for our sailor-lad. Jack alone was able to relate what had passed.

"Oh!" he said, "I have kissed their corpses," and a tear rolled down his sun-browned cheek.

He spoke of the dead bodies of Orazio and Irene, who loved him so much, and who had been his preservers. They had been removed for burial along with the other sad relics of our noble friends.

The women embraced, weeping on each other's bosoms, but unable to articulate a word. After assisting at this mute scene for some time, and showing himself also much affected, Captain Thompson raised his head, and, approaching his mistress, addressed her, cap in hand, saying—

"Madam, the yacht is anchored off the pier, awaiting your orders; do you desire to go on board?"

"Yes, Thompson," she replied, "let us go on board, and set sail immediately, so as to get out of Italy; it has become the grave of all its best and most beautiful."

Julia sailed for merry England, and took kind care of her adopted family, to whom were added, after a time, Manlio and Silvia. Until they joined her in England, they had remained on the island of the Recluse.

She vowed she would not return to that unhappy country until Rome, freed from priestly despotism, would permit her to raise a worthy national monument to her heart's beloved, and to his heroic companions.

APPENDIX.

—◆—

THE CAMPAIGN OF MENTANA.

By Ricciotti Garibaldi.

Arriving in Florence I found the committee in a state of confusion on account of so many volunteers coming forward to be enrolled. We had neither arms nor money, and were, therefore, obliged to limit enlistment. I remained three days in Florence, and then went to Terni, and found the place full of volunteers—in all nearly 2,000 men. We received information that the fortress occupied by Menotti was to be attacked. I left to join him, and the men, being unarmed, went alone.

He had 1,500 men. On the morning of the third day he left N—— with a few men, and went to Monte Calvario, leaving me in command of the fort and of the band, which had been reinforced by nearly 1,000 men. About eleven at night, on the same day, my outposts were driven in by the Papal troops. Many of our volunteers not having so much as one cartridge per man, I was obliged to abandon the fortress, and take up position to the left, at a distance of two miles, as it was impossible to hold the post against the Papal artillery. Menotti having rejoined us, we started, at one on the following morning, for Porcile, as the enemy were trying to cut us off from the Italian frontier. After twelve hours' march we arrived at Porcile. We rested there for the remainder of the day and night, when the alarm was given of the approach of the enemy. Being in an unfit state to receive them, with few arms and no ammunition, my brother determined to re-cross the frontier. After ten hours' march, we arrived at the convent of Santa Maria, where we set to work to re-form our command.

Whilst there news came that the General was at Terni, whence he sent orders for us to prepare to march on Passo Corese, he joining us on the road. This is a pass leading to the valley of the Tiber. After waiting several days to re-form the bands, the General gave the signal to march. We divided into two columns, and took the road to Monte Rotondo, a strong position occupied by the Papal troops. One column marched along the banks of the Tiber, and the other by the road in the hills. At morning both columns arrived in sight of Monte Rotondo, and at once proceeded to the assault. Colonel Frygisi attacked the east gateway with two battalions, whilst Masto attacked the west gateway also with two battalions; but he being wounded at the first assault, the command of the party devolved upon me. After charging twice up to the gateway, which, for want of artillery, we could not take, we were in turn attacked by the enemy, and forced to seek refuge in a group of houses. We were thus cut off from the rest of our corps for the whole day, during which time we lost out of 300, 107 men and 5 officers. In the evening we managed to communicate with the General; erected barricades in the inner street, and fought all day. We were thirty-six hours without food. The place was too important to be left, or we might have cut our way out. The General sent a battalion as a reinforcement, and by a desperate charge we got to the gate, piled there a cart-load of fusines and a quantity of sulphur, which, being set on fire, burnt it down in about an hour and a half. At half-past twelve at night—the General having come down and taken personal command—we charged through the burning gate, and took possession of the entrance and adjoining houses. The fighting went on until about eight in the morning, they defending themselves step by step till we had driven them into the palace of the Prince of Piombino, a large castellated building, very strong. We first took the court-yard, in which we found their cannon, they defending storey after storey of the building until driven to the third floor, when, seeing the smoke of a fire which had been lighted on the ground floor to burn them out, they surrendered, and the fight was over.

In the night the greater number of the men escaped towards Rome; only 300 in the palace were taken prisoners, besides forty-two horses and two pieces of cannon, 500 stand of arms, and all their materials of war. The fight had lasted twenty-four hours—from eight one day to eight the next—without a single instant's cessation of firing. It cost us between 400 and 500 men, amongst whom were some of our bravest and best officers.

This was the first real struggle under the General.

We had one day's rest; but on the following night the enemy returned, and attacked the railway station at about a mile distant from Monte Rotondo, where, finding a number of our wounded, they bayoneted them in their beds, one man having twenty-seven wounds in his body. The General at once sent heavy reinforcements, and the enemy was driven back. Three days after this we marched to the Zechinella, a large farm-house about a mile distant from the Ponte de la Mentana, within about four miles and a half from Rome. On our approach the enemy re-crossed the bridge, blowing up one of the two bridges, and mining the other. The Papal troops came again on our side of the Teverone—a river which joins the Tiber a few miles from Rome. They extended themselves as sharpshooters all along our line, amusing themselves by firing at us until the evening, we scarcely returning a shot, the General having ordered us not to do so— our aim, since we were so few, being to draw the enemy into the open country. In the night we lighted large fires, to let the people in Rome know that we were near; but the movement which we expected in the city did not take place, and we returned to Monte Rotondo the next day.

After staying there for several days, the General resolved to march to Tivoli, which was held by a strong body of our volunteers. The column, consisting of 4,700 infantry, two field guns and two smaller guns, and one squadron of cavalry, commenced its march at eleven o'clock. When we had gone a mile beyond Mentana the vanguard was suddenly attacked, and we had to fall back on Mentana, so as to form our battalions in line of battle. Recovered from our first surprise, the General ordered all the troops to advance, and we re-took the positions we had lost, when, just as the Papal troops were retreating on the road to Rome, the French regiments, which till now had remained hidden behind the hills, out-flanked us on the left. After some very heavy fighting, especially in the position of the haystacks in the centre, which were taken, lost, and re-taken, four or five times, the General seeing the uselessness of contending against such an overwhelming force, gave the order to retreat. We retreated from the field of battle, passing under the fire of the Chassepôts, leaving between 400 and 500 men on the field, and about the same number of prisoners in their hands, and one piece of cannon. Two battalions, numbering altogether over 400 men, shut themselves up in the old fort of Munturra, where, having exhausted all their ammunition, they surrendered in the morning. When the main body had returned to Monte Rotondo, the General gave orders that everything should be ready to re-attack in the night; but on examining the state of our army, we found that scarcely a cartridge remained, and not a single round of ammunition for the cannon. Learning this, the General gave the order to retreat to Passo Corese, where we arrived about one in the morning, being again on Italian soil. We then proceeded to the disbandment of our troops.

At Mentana, where we had retaken all our positions, and where we thought the day was ours, we saw red-trowsered soldiers out-flanking us on the left, and we took them for the legion of Antibes, but the rapid roll of their firing opened our eyes to the fact that we were face to face with the French, armed with their new weapon, the deadly Chassepôt, and from that moment we fought merely to save the honour of the day. There was no hope of winning the battle, though if the ammunition of our guns and rifles had not failed, and the General could have attacked again in the night, as he intended to do, I have no doubt but that we should have driven back the Franco-Papal army, for they did not dare to take possession of the positions which we held during the battle, and of the one gun which we left there till late next day. Had they dared it, being so numerically superior, they could have cut us off and made us all prisoners, as their left wing almost touched the road running from Monte Rotondo to Passo Corese.

Some idea may be formed of the state and appearance of the volunteer army by the fact that it had no proper arms ; the muskets were many of them as old as the first Napoleon.

When Menotti resolved to re-cross the frontier, he issued an order of the day in which he said : "I cannot march, having no shoes ; I cannot stand still, because I have nothing to cover my men ; and I cannot fight, because I have no ammunition."

When we started for Monte Rotondo the men had been so long without eating, that in passing along the line with my guides, I actually saw the infantry battalions making themselves soup out of the grass of the field, having nothing else to put into their cauldrons.

At the battle of Mentana we had 4,700 men all told ; opposed to us were 8,000 Papal troops and 3,000 French. Battle began at half-past eleven in the morning ; lasted until half-past five in the evening ;

the weather fine. The 300 who surrendered were allowed to re-cross the frontier. The General was taken prisoner by the Italian Government.

At Mentana the Papal troops thought they had taken me. They took a man like me to Rome, and put him in handsome apartments until the mistake was discovered. When they thought they had me the Papal officers ordered the prisoner to be shot at once, but the French officers saved him.

In a work entitled "Rome and Mentana," surprise has been expressed that General Garibaldi did not enter Rome after the victory of Monte Rotondo, and before the entry of the French. To that we reply :— We could not, for the Papalini held the Mentana bridge, the only one not blown up near Rome, and we should have been obliged to go round by Tivoli and down the other side of the Tenerone, two days' march. We tried to take the Mentana bridge, but on nearing it we found it strongly fortified and mined, so that after lying at the Zechinella (three-quarters of a mile from the bridge) for a day and two nights, we retired to Monte Rotondo.

The same work states :—

"The two plateaux on which we had been walking had been held by the Garibaldini, taken by the Pontificals, and re-taken by the Garibaldini, at which period the French advanced, when, finding it hopeless, the Garibaldini retreated into Mentana."

This is true ; the Papalini were retreating along the road when the French out-flanked our left, and threatened our line of retreat. The retreat commenced at nine o'clock in the evening of the battle, as we expected the Papalini to attack and surround Monte Rotondo. If we had stopped they would have made us all prisoners, as our ammunition failed.

We entered Monte Rotondo by the gate coming from Passo Corese ; the Tivoli gate was stormed also by Frigysi, but not taken till we opened the gate for him from inside. The attack lasted from 8 A.M. till

7 A.M. next day. We set fire to the gate about twelve o'clock at night, and lost about 250 men, dead and wounded. The church of Monte Rotondo suffered a good deal.

GARIBALDI AND THE ITALIAN GOVERNMENT.

ITALY, as she exists, is a sad country. Where is there to be found a country more favoured by nature, with a lovelier sky, a climate more salubrious, productions more varied and excellent, a population more lively or intelligent? Her soldiers, if well directed, would undoubtedly equal any of the first soldiers in the world; her sailors are second to none. And yet all these advantages, all these favours of Nature, are neutralised by the connivance and co-operation of priests with an extremely bad Government.

One finds misery, ignorance, weakness, servility to the foreigner, where one should see abundance, knowledge, strength, and haughtiness towards intruders.

An unpopular Government, which, instead of organising a national army that might be placed at the head of the first armies of the world, contents itself with accumulating many carbineers, policemen, and custom-house officers, and spending, or, rather, squandering the money of the nation in immoral "secret expenses." A navy that might compete with the most flourishing, is reduced to a pitiable condition from its being placed under the direction of incompetent and dishonest persons. Both army and navy, according to their own officers, are not in a condition to make war, but only serve to repress any national aspirations, and to support the spiritless policy of the government.

Two abominable acts of treachery have been perpetrated by the Italian Government.

The first act of treachery was ushered in by the arrest of General Garibaldi at Asinalunga. Eighteen

years had passed away since the Roman people sent to
the Quirinal their elected representatives, who, on the
9th of February, declared with solemn legality that the
temporal power of the Pope was abolished. The
patriots in public assembly, in the light of day, and
from the height of the Quirinal, unfurled the beautiful,
the holy, and beloved banner of the tricolour of Italy.
Who quenched this patriotic fire? A Buonaparte in
secret alliance with the fugitives of Gaeta. While the
balls of the French cannons fell on the citizens posted
at the barricades, the representatives of the people
replied to these cruel shots by again proclaiming the
statute of the Republic, and confiding the future
liberties of Rome to the charge of Garibaldi.

On September 16th, 1864, was concluded the per-
nicious convention of September, which the Moderates
declared would open the gates of Rome. Its first
result was that Turin saw its streets reddened with
blood. Why were the arms of their brothers turned
upon the people who deserved so well of Italy? Did
they wish to overthrow the dynasty? Did they wish
to overthrow the form of government, or overturn the
Ministers? Did they wish to upset social order?
Did they arm themselves against their brethren of the
army? Oh, no! they did not arm; they united
peaceably, and peaceably cried for justice. Their cry
was, "Rome the capital of Italy." They did not wish
the nation to betray itself; they did not wish the
nation to be dismembered; they did not wish the
country any longer to serve the foreigner. Its protest
was, therefore, against that convention which destroys
the plebiscite of Southern Italy. To the noble cry,
to the generous protest, the Government replied by
directing its troops upon the peaceful citizens; and the
Piazza Castello and the Piazzo San Carlo were bathed
in blood. Unhappy Turin! the Moderate party stifled
thy cries in thine own blood, betrayed thy solemn
protests, called upon thee not to disturb the concord of
the nation, and to that false concord sacrificed thee

and the nation alike. Widows and orphans well remember the impunity given to the assassins of their loved ones in the name of "concord." When will these crimes end? Without Rome, unity is for ever menaced. Without Rome, we have neither moral nor political liberty. We have no independence, no right government; but we have anarchy, dilapidation, servitude to the foreigner, and submission to the priests.

The Moderates acknowledge Cavour as their leader: hear, then, Cavour.

The Italian Parliament, in 1861, when Cavour was Prime Minister, declared Victor Emanuel King of Italy, and declared Rome officially the seat of the new monarchy; and Cavour stated, in his place as Prime Minister, after having bestowed upon the question the utmost deliberation, that "the ideas of a nation were few in number, and that to the common Italian mind the idea of Italy was inseparable from that of Rome. An Italy of which Rome was not the capital would be no Italy for the Italian people. For the existence, then, of a national Italian people, the possession of Rome as a capital was an essential condition." "The choice of a capital," continued Cavour, "must be determined by high moral considerations, on which the instinct of each nation must decide for itself. Rome, gentlemen, unites all the historical, intellectual, and moral qualities which are required to form the capital of a great nation. Convinced, deeply convinced as I am of this truth, I think it my bounden duty to proclaim it as solemnly as I can before you and before the country. I think it my duty also to appeal, under these circumstances, to the patriotism of all the Italian citizens, and of the representatives of our most illustrious cities, when I beg of them to cease all discussion on this question, so that Europe may become aware that the necessity of having Rome for our capital is recognised and proclaimed by the whole nation."

How the Moderates followed this advice has been already seen. But statements were circulated in their papers, far and wide, in order to reconcile the Italian people to a convention, that the rights of the Roman people would not be interfered with ; and when the French troops had left, the people of Rome would have full liberty to act as they thought proper. It was in this view that General Garibaldi visited Ovieto shortly before his arrest, where he was received with the most unbounded enthusiasm, the entire city being in festive garb, whilst men, women, and children joined in according him an enthusiastic welcome.

" Our cry must no longer be ' Rome or death ! ' " he said ; " on the contrary, it is ' Rome and life ! ' for international right permits the Roman to rise, and will allow them to raise themselves from the mud into which the priests have thrown them."

It was at four o'clock on Tuesday morning, on the 5th of September, that General Garibaldi was arrested, by order of Ratazzi, in the little village of Asinalunga. He was sleeping in the house of Professor Aqualucci, and he was, as the map will show, far from the Roman frontier. He had been received with the utmost respect by the syndic and by the secretary of the municipality, and all the usual rejoicings took place, though it is stated that all the time the syndic had the order for the General's arrest in his pocket. General Garibaldi was conveyed to the fortress of Alexandria. In a day or two he was informed that he would be entirely restored to liberty if he would consent to go to Caprera ; he had full liberty to return to the mainland whenever he thought proper. Depending upon this ministerial assurance, he returned to Caprera, having previously assured his friends in Genoa that he was in full and perfect liberty. An Italian fleet was sent to guard Caprera, and on his attempting to leave the island to go on board the Rubeatini postal steamers, his boat was fired at. He was taken on board a man-of-war, and conducted back to Caprera.

Then it was that, on the evening of the 14th of October, 1867, three individuals came down from the farm at Caprera towards Fontanazia; a fourth passed by way of the wooden porch which joins the small iron cottage to the large house, and took the high road to Stagnatia—the latter, by his dark physiognomy and the style of his apparel, appeared to be a Sardinian— the men belonging to the yacht which the munificence and sympathy of the generous English nation had placed at the disposal of the General. The first three men might have been recognised by that famous distinction, the red shirt, had not this garment, in a great measure, been concealed by the outer habiliments of each. They were Barberini and Fruchianti, and the third we need not describe. Barberini, though not strong by nature, had a wiry arm and the heart of a lion; Fruchianti was far more robust.

The scirocco, with its melancholy breath, beat down the poor plants of the island daughter of the volcanos and of the sea, and dense black clouds, chased by the impetuous winds, eddied on the summit of Veggialone, and then became mingled with dense vapours, which on higher mountains often form the centre of storms.

The three silent men descended, and on the way, whenever the unequal ground permitted a view of the port, they gazed with watchful eyes on the three ships which rocked gracefully in the Bay of Stagnabella. The yacht, with a small cannon at her bow, and a boat lashed to the poop, formed a strange contrast (completely deserted as she was) with the men of war, their decks covered and encumbered with men.

It was six o'clock in the evening, and the sun had set, and the night promised, if not tempest, that disagreeable and oppressive weather which the scirocco generally brings from the burning plains of the desert. The three men having arrived on the Prato, Fruchianti said, "I leave you; I am going to the left to explore the point of Araccio."

The two continued to descend; they passed—opening and shutting them again—the four gates of Fontanazia.

and arrived under the dry wall which divides the culti-
vated part from the deserted shores.

Having crossed the wall, and turned to Barberini,
the General (who had changed his white hat for a
cap) said, " Let us sit down and smoke half a cigar,"
and drawing from his left pocket a little case, a
souvenir from the amiable Lady Shaftesbury, he lit
one, which he then handed to his companion, a great
amateur of such commodities.

" In three-quarters of an hour," said the General,
"the moon will rise above the mountains, and there
is no time to lose."

Thereupon the two men took their way to the port.
Giovanni was at his post, and, with the aid of Barberini, in a moment the little skiff was in the water,
and the General sat on his cloak as low as possible.
After launching the little boat into the sea, Giovanni
embarked in the larger one, and having assured himself of the progress of the first, he proceeded towards
the yacht merrily singing.

" Halt ! who goes there ?" twice cried the men-of-
war's men who had become policemen to the Sardinian ruler. But he sang on, and did not seem to
care for their cries. Nevertheless, at the third intimation, Giovanni replied, "Going on board !" At
this they seemed satisfied.

Meanwhile the little skiff pursued her course, coasting Carriano, at the distance of two miles from the shore,
partly propelling itself, and partly propelled by a boat-
hook used in the American fashion. From Carriano to
Barabruciata, and thence to the point of Treviso, near
which appeared the form of the faithful Fruchianti.

" Nothing new as far as the rocks of Araccio," said
Fruchianti.

" Then I push on," answered the General.

And his little boat dashed among the breakers.
He gave a glance to the small island, which appeared at a convenient distance, and the tiny skiff
was on the high sea.

Garibaldi, seeing the moonlight increase, paddled on with good will, and with the help of the breeze crossed the Straits of Moneta with surprising velocity.

In the moonlight, at a certain distance, every reef appeared a boat; and as the squadron of Ratazzi, besides so many launches for the ships of war about Caprera, was also augmented by numerous vessels from Maddalena, the sea all around the island was crowded with vessels, to prevent one man from fulfilling his duty. Nearing the coast of the little island of Giardinelli, not far from Maddalena, the skiff plunged among the waters, which are always broken there, and coasted the shore, already illumined by the moon.

One must not ascribe all the merit to him who managed the boat, but much to the sleeping vigilance of those whose duty it was to have kept a better look-out, that he reached the little island safe and sound, without being molested by one solitary call of " Who goes there ? "

Having reached land, there were three paths to take : first, to row close to the land ; secondly, to leave the island to the left, and coast along to the west ; and thirdly, leaving the island to the right and following the coast, to approach the ford which separates it from Maddalena, where probably Basso and Captain Cunio were waiting. The first plan was adopted.

After having drawn up the boat on the beach, the General proceeded at mid-day in the direction of the ford, where, on his arrival, he heard cries from those who guarded the strait, and a few shots fired in the distance.

At a short distance from the ford of the island there is a wall covered with creepers, which prevents the escape of the animals that pasture in the island ; and at mid-day he reached a compound. Then also came the ford, and through the wall there was a little passage formed of stones.

The General thought he could distinguish along the
wall a file of sailors lying down, and he was so much
the more disposed to believe it, as Captain Cunio and
Basso had seen seamen arrive on the island in the
course of the day.   This made him lose about half an
hour waiting and reconnoitring, and Captain Cunio
and Basso, imagining the shots directed at the boat,
had concluded him taken or obliged to recede.   Under
this persuasion the friends returned from the ford
towards Maddalena, and were greatly vexed when,
towards 2 P.M., they were informed by the confidential
servant of Mrs. Collins that he, the General, had
reached her house.   In fact, about 10 P.M., Garibaldi
ventured to pass the little strait which divides the isle
from Maddalena, and effected it without hindrance,
but was obliged, to his great inconvenience, to ride a
long way down a road flooded with water, which had
deluged it.   He then came in sight of Mrs. Collins's
house, sure of a good reception, but drew near cautiously,
apprehending that some one might be on the watch;
and finally, in a moment in which the moon was
veiled by a dark cloud, he approached the dwelling,
and with the end of his Scotch walking-stick tapped at
the window.

Mrs. Collins, who had strong faith in the fortunes
of the General, and who was warned of his attempt,
expected him, so that at the first sound she advanced
to the front door, opened it, and received her old
neighbour with friendly greetings.   And pleasant he
found it to receive shelter after such a wild night ; so
that the wanderer was once more safe and indeed
happy in his friend's house, where a thousand cares
and attentions were lavished on him.

After this there was a little difficulty in crossing
Sardinia and reaching the mainland.   While the
Government still supposed Garibaldi a prisoner at
Caprera, he had arrived in safety at the Hôtel de
Florence !

Not less atrocious was the treachery used towards

the volunteers. They were promised that as soon as the first French soldier disembarked, the army should march on Rome, and the Government, to put the country off her guard, occupied several points of the Roman territory, and spread a considerable number of troops over the frontier, that they might the more easily disarm the volunteers, as well as close up from them every path, so that no supplies or subsidies could reach them from their brothers and the Committee of Help.

Having thus isolated the volunteers, and deprived them of succour and supplies—especially the supply of ammunition, of which the Government knew them to be in want—they spread discouragement and demoralisation among the young volunteers, and did all they could to betray and destroy them.

Rome being occupied by the French, and part of the Roman territory by the Government troops, the Papal army *en masse* could freely operate against the volunteers. The Papal mercenaries, still alarmed by the recent defeats they had sustained, did not dare to confront alone the unarmed soldiers of liberty, and it was therefore determined that the French army should support the Papal troops.

The Government of Florence did not think it necessary to take part in the glory of the battle of Mentana, by adding its troops to those of the French allies ; or perhaps it believed, and with reason, that the Italian people would not have quite tolerated such an accumulation of villainy, although the Ministry would certainly have executed it of themselves without any remorse. It contented itself, therefore, with depriving the volunteers of their natural aids, with sowing diffidence and discouragement in the hearts of our youthful and impressible soldiers, and with giving the National Army Contingent orders to slaughter the flower of the Italian nation, their brother Italians.

Well was it for the soldiers of the Pope that they were backed by those of Buonaparte.

The battle of Mentana commenced at 1 P.M. on the 3rd of November, between the Papal troops and the volunteers. After two hours' desperate fighting the mercenaries' lines had all fallen back, and our men marched over their corpses in pursuit of the fugitives. But the new line of Imperialists advancing, and finding our youthful volunteers in that disorder incidental under these circumstances to men little disciplined, compelled them to retreat.

In this manner was accomplished two most execrable acts of treachery, to which parallels cannot be found in any page of the world's history.

NOTES.

NOTE 1, PAGE 4, VOL. I.

Among the cardinals nominated by Sixtus IV. was
Raffaelle, who, under the direction of his great-uncle,
Sixtus IV., had acted the principal part in the bloody
conspiracy of the Pazza. In assuming his seat among the
fathers of the Christian Church, Giovanni de Medici, afterwards Leo X., found himself associated with one who had
assisted in the murder of his uncle, and had attempted the
life of his father. But the youth and inexperience of Riaro
excused the enormity of a crime perpetrated under the
sanction of the supreme pontiff.

The eldest member of the college at this time was
Roderigo Borgia, who had enjoyed for upwards of thirty-
five years the dignity of the purple, to which he had for a
long time past added that of the vice-chancellor to the holy
see.

The private life of Roderigo had been a perpetual disgrace
to his ecclesiastical functions. In the Papal His ory by
Dr. Beggi (edition 1862, pages 553—556) we are told that
this cardinal was at one time sovereign regent of Rome,
that he had a ferocious and indomitable ambition, with
such a perverse spirit fomented by debauchery, luxury, and
riches, that in the contempt of any pretence of virtue, he
lived publicly with a barefaced concubine named Rosa
Vennozza, by whom he had many children. After his
election to the chair of St. Peter, he created his eldest son
Duke of Candia. Cæsar Borgia was the second son;
Lucretia Borgia was of the same stock, and the eldest of
several daughters whom he had by other mistresses.

On the death of Inuocent VIII., Cardinal Roderigo
Borgia, being the most powerful in authority and wealth,
with cunning artifices, and corrupt promises to the Roman
barons and the most influential cardinals—such as the
Sforzas, the Orsini, the Riarii, and others—ascended the
papal chair under the title of Alexander VI.

NOTE 2, PAGE 7, VOL. I.

A better illustration of the manner in which the Church of Rome applies her patronage of the fine arts to the inculcation of her doctrines and the increase of her power, can hardly be found than among the frescoes of the Campo Santo, Pisa. Here we have represented the most ghastly cartoons of death, judgment, purgatory, and hell; we behold angels and devils fighting for the souls of the departed, snakes devouring, fiends scorching, red-hot hooks tearing their flesh. Those on earth can, so say the priests, rescue their unfortunate relatives from this melancholy position by giving donations to their spiritual fathers, who will then pray for their escape. We read in the New Testament that the rich enter heaven with difficulty, but it is they, according to the Church of Rome, who enter easily, whilst the poor are virtually excluded.

NOTE 3, PAGE 8, VOL. I.

In foreign discussions on the papal question it is always assumed as an undisputed fact that the maintenance of the papal court at Rome is, in a material point of view, an immense advantage to the city, whatever it may be in a moral one. Now my own observations have led me to doubt the correctness of this assumption. If the Pope were removed from Rome, or if a lay government were established—the two hypotheses are practically identical—the number of the clergy would undoubtedly be much diminished, a large number of the convents and clerical endowments would be suppressed, and the present generation of priests would be heavy sufferers. This result is inevitable. Under no free government would or could a city of 170,000 inhabitants support 10,000 unproductive persons out of the common funds—for this is substantially the case in Rome at the present day. Every sixteen lay citizens—men, women, and children—support out of their labour a priest between them. The papal question with the Roman priesthood is thus a question of daily bread, and it is surely no want of charity to suppose that the material aspect influences their minds quite as much as the spiritual. It is, however, a Protestant delusion that the priests of Rome live upon the fat of the land. What fat there is is certainly theirs. It is one of the mysteries of Rome how the hundreds of priests who swarm about the streets manage to live. The clue to the mystery is to be found inside the churches. In every church—and there are 366 of them—some score or two of masses are said daily at the different altars. The pay for performing a mass varies from sixpence to five shillings. The good masses—those paid for by private persons for the souls of their relatives—are naturally reserved for the priests connected with a particular church ; while the poor ones are given to any priest who happens to apply for them. The nobility, as a body, are sure to be the supporters of an established order of things ; their interests, too, are very much mixed up with those of the papacy. There is not a single noble Roman family that has not one or more of its members among the higher ranks of the priesthood. And in a considerable degree their distinctions, such as they are, and their temporal prospects, are bound up with the popedom. Moreover, in this rank of the social scale the private and personal influence of the priests through the women of the family is very powerful. The more active, however, and ambitious amongst the aristocracy feel deeply the exclusion from public life, the absence from any opening for ambition, and the gradual impoverishment of their property, which are the necessary evils of an absolute ecclesiastical government.—*Dicey's " Rome in 1860."*

Note 4, Page 155, Vol. I.

The Moderates.—An attempt has recently been made to give to the so-called Moderate party the merit of planning a United Italy. Mr. Stansfeld, one of the Lords of the Admiralty, whose recent efforts to reform his department have already earned for him the gratitude of the English people, says, " Italy has already accomplished of her unity so much that no policy save that of an absolute completion of the task is any longer to be dreamed of or suggested, and considering, too, how predominantly the credit and the practical fruits of that success have, in the opinion of the world contributed to the benefit of the Moderate party, it would seem natural to imagine that they too must have had the unity of their country long in view, and that they can have differed only from the National party as to the policy best adapted to the attainment of a common object; and yet I believe the acceptance of the idea of Italian unity, as an object of practical statesmanship, by the leaders of the Moderate party, must be admitted to be of a very recent date. I will go back to Gioberti, who was the founder of that party. In the Sardinian Chambers on the 10th of February, 1849, on the eve of the short campaign which ended in the defeat of Novara, Gioberti said—' I consider the unity of Italy a chimera; we must be content with its union.' And if you look to the writings, the speeches, the acts, of all the leading men of the Moderate party until a very recent period, you will find them all, without exception, not only not propounding or advocating unity, or arts, directed to its accomplishment, but explicitly directed to a different solution. You will find the proof of what I say in Balbo's "Hopes of Italy;" in Durando's "Essay on Italian Nationality," advocating three Italies, north, centre, and south; in Bianchi Giovini's work entitled "Mazzini and his Utopias;" and in Gualterio's "Revolutions of Italy." Minghetti, Ricasoli, Farini, each and all have been the advocates of a confederation of Princes rather than of a united Italy. Let me come to Cavour. An attempt has recently been made to claim for him the credit of having since the days of his earliest manhood conceived the idea of making himself the minister of a future united Italy. In an article in the July *Quarterly* by a well-known pen, a letter of Cavour, written about 1829 or 1830, is cited in implied justification of this claim. He had been placed under arrest a short time in the Fort de Bard, on account of political opinions expressed with too much freedom. In a letter to a lady who had written condoling with him on his disgrace, he says:—"I thank you, Madame la Marquise, for the interest which you take in my disgrace; but believe me, for all that, I shall work out my career. I have much ambition—an enormous ambition; and when I become minister I hope to justify it, since already in my dreams, I see myself Minister of the Kingdom of Italy." Now this is, I need not say, a most remarkable letter, and of the greatest interest, as showing the confidence in his own future, at so early an age, of one of the greatest statesmen of our times. But no one acquainted with the modern history of Italy, and familiar with its recognised phraseology, could read in this letter the prophecy of that unity which is now coming to pass. The "Kingdom of Italy" is a well-known phrase borrowed from the time of Napoleon, and has always meant, until facts have enlarged its significance, that the kingdom of northern Italy, whose precedent existed under Napoleon, which was the object of Piedmontese policy in '48 and '49, and one of the explicit terms of the contract of Pombier's in '59. It is rather a curious inconsistency in the article in question, that in itself furnishes ample evidence that the unity of Italy was not part of the practical programme of the Moderate party. "Cavour," we are told, "founded in 1847 with his friends, Cesare Baldo, Santa Rosa, Buoncampagni, Castelli, and other men of moderate constitutional views, the *Risorgimento*, of which he became the editor; and the principles of the new periodical were announced to be 'Independence of Italy,' union between the princes,' and the people's progress in the path of reform, and a league between the Italian States." Again, after saying that it was Ricasoli and the leaders of the constitutional party who recalled (in '49) the Grand Ducal family to Tuscany, and that Gioberti proposed the return of the Pope to Rome, the writer goes on to say, "It was an immense advantage to the restored princes to have been thus brought back by the most intelligent and moderate of their subjects. All that the wisest and most influential men in Italy asked, was a federal union of the different states in the Peninsula, upon a liberal and constitutional basis, from which even the House of Austria was not to be excluded."

At the Conference of Paris in 1855, after the Crimean war, Piedmont was represented by Cavour, who brought before the assembled statesmen the condition of Italy, but unable to enter fully into the Italian question, he addressed two state papers on it to Lord Clarendon. His plan—at any rate, for the temporary settlement of the question—was a confederation of Italian States with constitutional institutions, and a guarantee of complete independence from the direct interference and influence of Austria; and the secularisation of the legations with a lay vicar under the suzerainty of the Pope. At that time he would have been even willing to acquiesce in the occupation of Lombardy by Austria, had she bound herself to keep within the limits of the treaty of 1815.

Now you cannot, I think, have failed to note the glaring inconsistency of the praises of what is called the moderation of Cavour, with the assumption to him and to his party of the whole credit of Italian unity, and the theory, now too prevalent, that no other party has contributed anything but follies and excesses, impediments, not aids, to the accomplishment of the great task. I believe such ideas to be as profoundly ungenerous and unjust as they are evidently self-contradictory, and I believe that they will be adjudged by history to be, so far as they are in any degree in good faith, superficial, partial, and utterly incapable of serving as any explanation of the method of the evolution of the great problem of Italian nationality.

Now let another witness be called into court, the late Prime Minister of Italy, Farina, on the authority of the Turin *Times* correspondent, who wrote, September 12, 1861: "You have not forgotten that in the Æmilia, Farina used, with great bitterness, to complain of the worthlessness of the Moderate party in time of trial and strife."*—*From " Garibaldi and Italian Unity," by Lieut.-Col. Chambers,* 1864.

NOTE 5, PAGE 185, VOL. I.

Many of our readers may have only an indistinct idea of the causes which led to the siege of Rome in 1849; and to understand it we must turn for a moment to the history of France. The revolution of 1848, which dethroned Louis Philippe and the house of Orleans, and established a Republican Government in France, was the signal for a general revolutionary movement throughout Europe. The Fifth Article of the new French Constitution stated, " The French republic respects foreign nationalities. She intends to cause her own to be respected. She will never undertake any sin for the purpose of conquest, and will never employ her arms against the liberty of any people." Prince Louis Napoleon was elected a member of the Chambers. He had fought for the Italian liberty in the year 1831, when the Bolognese revolution broke out. Louis Napoleon had taken an active part in the campaign, and, aided by General Sercognani, defeated the Papal forces in several places. His success was of short duration. He was deprived of his command, and banished from Italy, and only escaped the Austrian soldiers by assuming the disguise of a servant.† When the prince landed in France from England, where he had resided several years, he caused a proclamation to be posted on the walls of Boulogne, from which we extract the following :—

"I have come to respond to the appeal which you have made to my patriotism. The mission which you impose on me is a glorious one, and I shall know how to fulfil it. Full of gratitude for the affection you manifest towards me, I bring you my whole life, my whole soul.

"Brothers and citizens, it is not a pretender whom you receive into your midst. I have not meditated in exile to

---

* Count Cavour wrote from Paris in 1856 to M. Ratazzi the following :—"I have seen Mr. Mauin. He is a very good man, but he always talks about the unity of Italy, and such other tomfooleries." Also La Larina, Cavour's agent in Italy in 1860, published in that year the following explanation of his differences with General Garibaldi :—He stated, " I believed, and still believe, that the only salvation for Sicily is the constitutional government of Victor Emmanuel." This explanation was published before Garibaldi crossed to the mainland ; and had Cavour gained his point, and obtained annexation, the kingdom of Naples would now have been under Bourbon rule.

† See " Vicissitudes of Families," by Sir Bernard Burke, pp. 291, 295. See also " The Autobiography of an Italian Rebel," by Riccalde, from p. 5.

no purpose. A pretender is a calamity. I shall never be ungrateful, never a malefactor. It is as a sincere and ardent Democratic Reformer that I come before you. I call to witness the mighty shade of the man of the age, as I solemnly make these promises:—

" I will be, as I always have been, the child of France.

" In every Frenchman I shall always see a brother.

" The rights of every one shall be my rights.

" The Democratic Republic shall be the object of my worship. I will be its priest.

" Never will I seek to clothe myself in the Imperial purple.

" Let my heart be withered within my breast on the day when I forget what I owe to you and to France.

" Let my lips be for ever closed if I ever pronounce a word, a blasphemy, against the Republican sovereignty of the French people.

" Let me be accursed on the day when I allow the propagation, under cover of my name, of doctrines contrary to the democratic principle which ought to direct the government of the Republic.

" Let me be condemned to the pillory on the day when, a criminal and a traitor, I shall dare to lay a sacrilegious hand on the rights of the people—whether by fraud, with its consent, or by force and violence against it."—See *Courrier de la Sarthe.*

And on December 2nd, 1848, he addressed the following letter to the Editor of the *Constitutionnel :—*

" MONSIEUR,

" Sachant qu'on a remarqué mon absence au vote pour l'expédition de Civita Vecchia, je crois devoir déclarer, que bien que résolu à appuyer toutes les dispositions propres à garantir la liberté et l'autorité du Souverain Pontife, je n'ai pu néanmoins approuver, par mon vote, une démonstration militaire qui me semblait périlleuse, même pour les intérêts sacrés que l'on veut protéger, et faite pour compromettre la paix européene.

(Signé) L. N. BUONAPARTE."

It must also be borne in mind that the Emperor Napoleon, his uncle, had created his own son King of Rome, and had detained the Pope a prisoner in France; when, therefore, Prince Louis Napoleon was elected President of the French Republic, it was universally supposed that he would rejoice at the formation of a sister Republic in the Roman States. The Roman Constituent Assembly elected by universal suffrage voted by one hundred and forty-three against five votes for the perpetual abolition of the temporal government of the Pope.

On the 18th of April, 1849, the Constituent Assembly voted that a manifesto should be addressed to the Governments and Parliaments of England and France. In this document it was stated, "That the Roman people had a right to give themselves the form of government which pleased them; that they had sanctioned the independence and free exercise of the spiritual authority of the Pope; and that they trusted that England and France would not assist in restoring a government irreconcilable by its nature with liberty and civilisation, and morally destitute of all authority for many years past, and materially so during the previous five months."

Notwithstanding this, the French Government despatched a French army to Civita Vecchia, where they landed on the 27th of April, 1849. General Oudinot declared that the flag which he had hoisted was that of peace, order, conciliation, and true liberty, and he invited the Roman people to co-operate in the accomplishment of this patriotic and sacred work. He also declared that the French had landed, not to defend the existing Pontifical Government, but to avert great misfortunes from the country. France, he added, did not arrogate to herself the right to regulate the interests which belonged to the Roman people and extended to the whole Christian world. The prefect of the province replied, "Force may do much in this world, but I am averse to believe that republican France will employ its troops to overthrow the rights of a republic formed under the same auspices as her own. I am convinced that when you ascertain the truth you will feel assured that in our country the republic is supported by the immense majority of the people."

The Roman Government—which was a Triumvirate consisting of Mazzini, Armellini, and Aurelio Saffi—resolved to oppose force by force, and the Assembly did not hesitate. The Triumvirate entrusted to General Garibaldi, who arrived the same evening, the defence of the city of Rome. It is impossible to describe the enthusiasm which took possession of the population at the sight of him. The courage of the people increased with their confidence, and it appeared as if the Assembly had not only decreed defence but victory.

Garibaldi upheld for three months in the future capital of the nation the national flag, against the forces of France, Austria, Naples, and Spain. Twice were the French troops attacked at the point of the bayonet and repulsed far beyond the walls. It was afterwards stated by French writers, that the French soldiers only intended to make a reconnaissance, and had fallen into a snare. This is not true. The French general had resolved upon a battle, the plan of which was found on the body of a French officer killed in the conflict, and transmitted to the Minister of War. It was after this victory that Garibaldi, seeing all the advantages of his situation, wrote to Avizzana, Minister of War : " Send me fresh troops, and as I promised to beat the French, and have kept my word, I promise you I will prevent any one of them from regaining their vessels." It was then that Mazzini, placing all his hopes on the French democratic party, of which Ledru-Rollin was the chief, interposed his authority. He refused the fresh troops asked for, and ordered Garibaldi not to make a mortal enemy of France by a complete defeat.

On Monday, 7th May, in the French National Assembly there was an animated discussion on the French expedition to Rome, M. Jules Favre having denounced its proceedings as contrary to the intention avowed by ministers, which was to prevent foreign interference at Rome, and as clearly opposed to the wishes of the Roman people ; he also stated, on the authority of private letters, that five unsuccessful assaults had been made, that 150 men had been killed and 600 wounded, and he ended by moving the appointment of a committee. M. Barrot, the President of the Council, declared that the object of the expedition was, really, to prevent another power from interfering in the affairs of Rome, and expressed his belief that General Oudinot had not acted contrary to his instructions, though the army might have fallen into a snare. He opposed the committee as unconstitutional, and called upon the assembly to reject the motion. General Lamoricière believed that General Oudinot might have been deceived as to the wishes of the people of Rome.

M. Flocon announced that barricades had been erected at Rome, and that the French residents would fight against the new-comers. After some further discussion, M. Barrot acquiesced in the motion, and the members withdrew to appoint the committee.

The sitting was resumed at nine o'clock, when the report of the committee was presented. It stated that as the idea of the Assembly had been that the expedition sent to Civita Vecchia ought to remain there, unless Austria moved on Rome, or a counter revolution in that city rendered an advance necessary, the committee considered that more had been done than had been intended, and it therefore proposed a resolution declaring that the National Assembly requested the Government to take measures that the expedition to Italy be no longer turned aside from its real object. M. Drouyn de Lhuys, on the part of the Government, said he must positively refuse to order the troops to return to Civita Vecchia, their presence being required by events at Rome. The minister further declared that the Government fully supported its agent, the gereral-in-chief, and the more so that the details of the encounter at Rome were wanting. M. Lenard accused the ministry of wishing to put down the Roman republic. After various amendments had been proposed and rejected, the resolution of the committee was carried against ministers by a majority of 328 to 241. The result was received with loud cheers, and cries of "Vive la République," and the Chamber adjourned at a quarter past one o'clock.

Notwithstanding this vote of the French National Assembly, the President of the Republic, Prince Louis Napoleon, addressed a letter to General Oudinot, in which he says: "I had hoped that the inhabitants of Rome would receive with eagerness an army which had arrived there to accomplish a friendly and disinterested mission. This has not been the case, our soldiers have been received as enemies, our military honour is engaged. I shall not suffer it to be assailed. Reinforcements shall not be wanting to you."

The envoy of the Roman Government in Paris, addressed the following letter, in the name of the Roman people, to their brothers in France: "A sanguinary combat has taken place between the inhabitants of Rome and the children of France, whom rigorous orders urged against our homes; the sentiment of military honour commanded them to obey their chiefs, the sentiment of patriotism ordered us to defend our liberties and our country. Honour is saved, but at what a price! may the terrible responsibility be averted from us, who are united by the bonds of charity! May even the culpable be pardoned; they are punished sufficiently by remorse. Health and fraternity.—L. TARPOLEI, Colonel, Envoy Extraordinary, of the Roman Republic in Paris."

In the next sitting of the French National Assembly, the subject of the President's letter to General Oudinot was brought forward by M. Grevy, in reply to whom M. Odillon Barrot stated that though the letter in question was not the act of the Cabinet, he and his colleagues were ready to assume the whole responsibility of it. He declared that the object of the letter was merely to express sympathy with the army, and that it was not intended as the inauguration of a policy contrary to that of the Assembly.

General Changarnier placed the letter of the President of the Republic to General Oudinot on the orders of the day of every regiment in the French service, although M. Odillon Barrot declared in the Assembly that it was not official. Also General Foret refused to obey the orders of the President of the Assembly by sending two battalions to guard it during its sitting—a breach of orders which was brought under the notice of the Assembly by M. Armand Manest, and apologised for by M. Odillon Barrot. On the 9th of May, M. Ledru-Rollin declared the letter of the President to General Oudinot to be an insolent defiance of the National Assembly, and a violation of the Constitution.

Ultimately the debate was adjourned on the motion of M. Grevy and M. Favre, in consequence of M. Odillon Barrot having announced that M. Lesseps, the late minister from Paris at Madrid, had been sent by the Government as an envoy to Rome to express to the Roman people the wishes of the Assembly, which showed that the Government did not intend to oppose the Assembly.

We will now return to Rome, and to the day of the first victory over the French. The joy which pervaded Rome in the evening and night which followed this first combat may be easily supposed. The whole city was illuminated, and presented the aspect of a national fête. Songs and bands of music were heard in all directions. The next day, the 1st of May, Garibaldi received from the Minister of War authority to attack the French with his legion. He took up a splendid position on a height on the flank of the French army; but at the moment the Italians were about to charge, a French officer arrived and demanded a parley with Garibaldi. He stated that he was sent by General Oudinot to treat for an armistice, and to be assured that the Roman people really accepted the Republican Government, and were determined to defend their rights. As a proof of his good intentions, the French General offered to give up Garibaldi's favourite chaplain, Ugo Bassi, who (having the evening before refused to leave a dying man whose head he was holding on his knees) had been taken prisoner.

The Roman Minister of War ordered Garibaldi to return to Rome, which he did, accompanied by a French officer. The armistice requested by General Oudinot was accorded by the Triumvirs, and the Republican Government granted unconditional liberty to fully 500 French prisoners in their hands. A letter from Garibaldi, after speaking of the bravery displayed by the Roman troops, says : " A quantity of arms, drums, and other matters have remained in our hands. The wounded French, before expiring, expressed their sorrow for having fought against their republican brethren."

The King of Naples, at the head of his army, was now marching upon Rome. Seeing this, Garibaldi, whom the armistice left unoccupied, demanded permission to employ his leisure in attacking the King of Naples. This permission was granted, and on the evening of the 4th of May Garibaldi left the city with his legion, now 2,500 strong.

On May 6th, General Garibaldi gained the battle of Palestrina, completely defeating the Neapolitans, 7,000 strong, and taking their artillery. Shortly after, however, the ambassador of the French Republic, Ferdinand de Lesseps, entered Rome with Michael Accrusi, the envoy of the Roman Republic in Paris, and by means of the good offices of the French Ambassador, the armistice, against which General Garibaldi had given a strong opinion, was concluded. The Roman Government resolved to take advantage of this truce to get rid of the Neapolitan army. At the same time Mazzini first created Colonel Roselli a general, and then named him general-in-chief of the forces. The friends of Garibaldi urged upon him not to accept a secondary position under a man who the day before only had been his inferior. The General, however, was utterly inaccessible to personal considerations where the welfare of his country was concerned, and he therefore accepted, he states himself, even with gratitude, the post of general of division.

On the 16th May the entire army of the Republic, consisting of 10,000 men and twelve pieces of cannon, marched out of the city of Rome by the San Giovanni gate, General Garibaldi being ordered to proceed in advance. He had received information that the Neapolitan army was encamped at Velletri, with 19,000 to 20,000 men and thirty pieces of cannon.

In the end the army of the King of Naples was again entirely defeated by General Garibaldi's division alone. In an early part of the day he sent to the commander-in-chief for reinforcements, and received for answer that soldiers could not be sent, as they had not eaten their soup. He then resolved to do what he could with his own strength, and victory again crowned his efforts. Towards midnight his troops took possession of Velletri itself.

At daybreak the General resumed the pursuit of the Neapolitans; but he received orders to return to Rome, which he re-entered on the 24th of May, amidst an immense multitude, who hailed him with the wildest cries of joy. The utter incapacity of General Roselli is now acknowledged by all; however, in those days, he shared the views of the Roman Government regarding the French.

In the meantime, General Oudinot, having received the reinforcements which he required, disavowed the treaty entered into by the Roman Government and the envoy extraordinary of his master the President of the French Republic. It would have been thought that the dream of a French alliance would now have faded from the ideas of the Roman Government, but they were only half convinced even yet, and they allowed their commander-in-chief, the newly created General Roselli, to indite a letter, from which the following is an extract:—

"General Oudinot, Duke de Reggio, citizen,—It is my perfect conviction that the army of the Roman Republic will one day fight side by side with the army of the French Republic to maintain the most sacred rights of peoples. This conviction leads me to make you proposals, which I hope you will accept. It is known to me that a treaty has been signed between the Government and plenipotentiary minister of France, a treaty which has not received your approbation." The letter goes on to request an unlimited armistice, with a notification of fifteen days before the resumption of hostilities, asked in the name of the honour of the army and of the French Republic, and concludes, "I have the honour to request a prompt reply, General, begging you to accept the salutation of fraternity.— ROSELLI."

To this the French general replied:—

"General,—The orders of my Government are positive. They prescribe to me to enter Rome as soon as possible. * * * I defer the attack of the place until Monday morning at least. Receive, General, the assurance of my high consideration.—The General-in-Chief of the corps de l'armée of the Mediterranean, Oudinot, Duc de Reggio."

According to this assurance the attack would not commence till the 4th of June.

"It is true," writes General Garibaldi, "what a French author, Foland, has said in his commentaries upon Polybius, 'A general who goes to sleep on the faith of a treaty awakes a dupe.' I was aroused at three o'clock by the sound of cannon: I found everything on fire. This is what had happened: Our advanced posts were at the Villa Pamphili. At the moment midnight was striking, and we were entering on the day of Sunday, the 3rd of June, a

French column glided through the darkness towards the Villa Pamphili. 'Who goes there?' cried the sentinel, warned by the sound of footsteps. 'Viva Italia!' cried a voice. The sentinel, thinking he had to do with compatriots, suffered them to approach, and was poniarded. The column rushed into the Villa Pamphili. All they met with were either killed or made prisoners. Some men jumped through the windows into the garden, and when once in the garden climbed over the walls. The most forward of them retired behind the convent of St. Pancrazio, shouting "To arms! to arms!" whilst others ran off in the direction of the Villas Valentini and Corsini. Like the Villa Pamphili, these were carried by surprise, but not without making some resistance.

"When I arrived at the St. Pancrazio gate, the Villa Pamphili, the Villa Corsini, and the Villa Valentini alone remained in our hands. Now the Villa Corsini being taken was an enormous loss to us; for as long as we were masters of that, the French could not draw their parallels. At any price, then, that must be re-taken: it was for Rome a question of life or death. The firing between the cannoneers of the ramparts, the men of the Vascello, and the French of the Villa Corsini and the Villa Valentini, increased. But it was not a fusillade or a cannonade that was necessary; it was an assault, a terrible but victorious assault, which might restore the Villa Corsini to us. For a moment the Villa Corsini was ours. That moment was short, but it was sublime! The French brought up all their reserve, and fell upon us altogether before I could even repair the disorder inseparable from victory. The fight was renewed more desperately, more bloodily, more fatally than ever. I saw re-pass before me, repulsed by the irresistible powers of war, fire and steel, those whom I had seen pass on but a minute before, now bearing away their dead.

"There could no longer be any idea of saving Rome. From the moment an army of 40,000 men, having thirty-six pieces of siege cannon, can perform their works of approach, the taking of a city is nothing but a question of time; it must one day or other fall. The only hope it has left is to fall gloriously. As long as one of our pieces of cannon remained on its carriage, it replied to the French fire; but on the evening of the 29th the last was dismounted."

Garibaldi was summoned before the Assembly, and this is his history of what happened:—

"Mazzini had already announced to the Assembly the

position we now stood in: there remained, he said, but three courses to take—to treat with the French; to defend the city from barricade to barricade; or to leave the city, assembly, triumvirate, and army, carrying away with them the palladium of Roman liberty.

"When I appeared at the door of the chamber all the deputies rose and applauded. I looked about me and upon myself to see what it was that awakened their enthusiasm. I was covered with blood; my clothes were pierced with balls and bayonet thrusts. They cried, 'To the tribune! to the tribune!' and I mounted it. I was interrogated on all sides.

"'All defence is henceforth impossible,' replied 1, 'unless we are resolved to make Rome another Saragossa.' On the 9th of February I proposed a military dictatorship, that alone was able to place on foot a hundred thousand armed men. The living elements still subsisted; they were to be sought for, and they would have been found in one courageous man. If I had been attended to, the Roman eagle would again have made its eyrie upon the towers of the Capitol; and with my brave men—and my brave men know how to die, it is pretty well seen—I might have changed the face of Italy. But there is no remedy for that which is done. Let us view with head erect the conflagration of which we no longer are the masters. Let us take with us from Rome all of the volunteer army who are willing to follow us. Where we shall be, Rome will be. I pledge myself to nothing; but all that my men can do that I will do—and whilst it takes refuge in us our country shall not die."

In the end the following order was issued:—

"The Roman Republic, in the name of God and the People. The Roman Constituent Assembly discontinues a defence which has become impossible. It has its post. The triumvirate are charged with the execution of the present decree."

END OF VOL. II.

CASSELL, PETTER, AND GALPIN, BELLE SAUVAGE WORKS, LONDON, E.C.

6 9 7 1 5 .